THE MEDALLION

Behind Blue Eyes Book 2

SARA J. BERNHARDT

First Edition

Behind Blue Eyes, book 2

2019 Lavish Publishing, LLC

Published in the United States by Lavish Publishing, LLC, Midland, TX

Cover Design by: Alexcia Productions

Cover Images: CANSTOCK

Paperback Edition

ISBN: 978-1-944985-71-4

www.LavishPublishing.com

Contents

"I want you to believe... to believe in things you cannot."

--Bram Stoker : Dracula

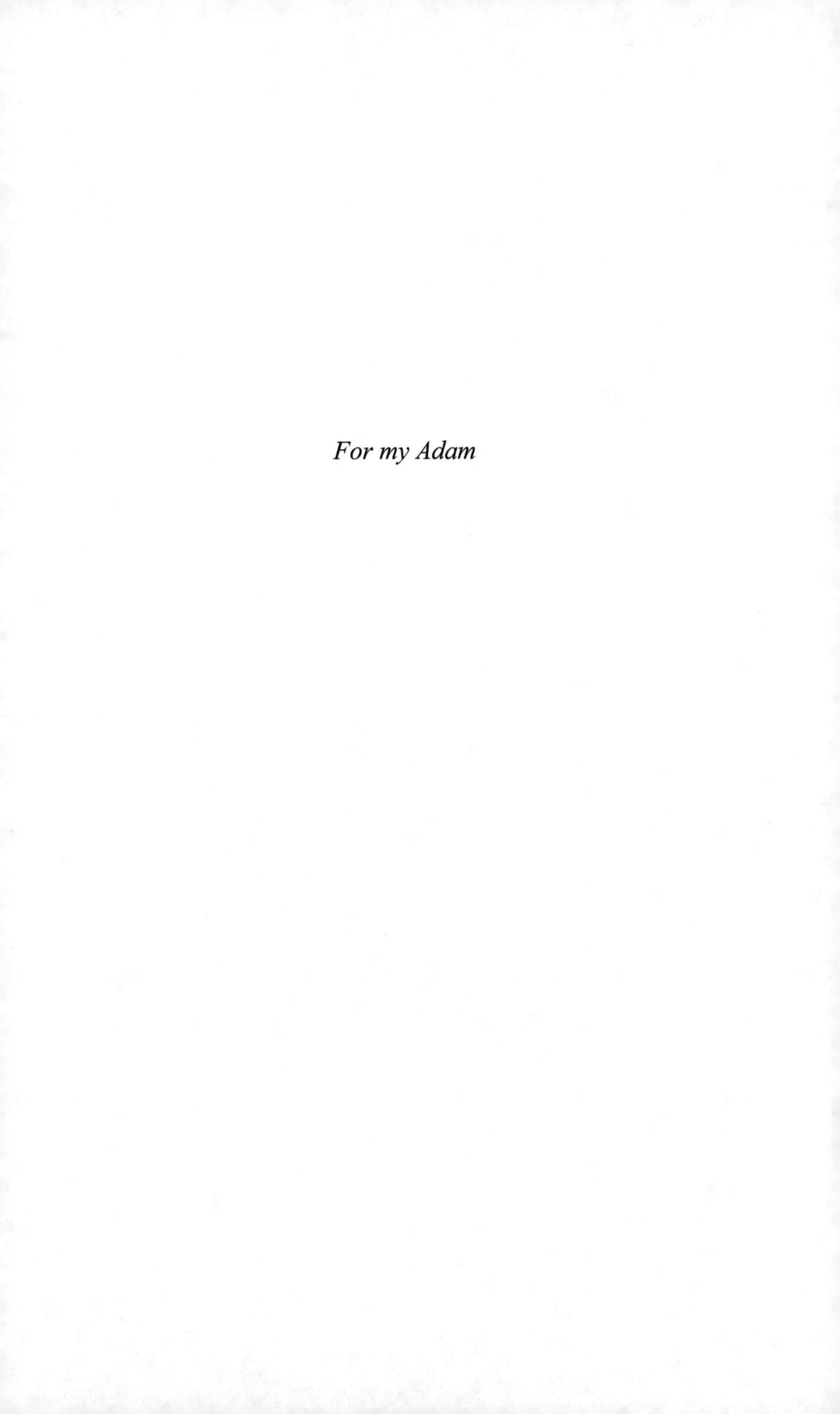

For my Adam

Chapter One

THE GUILT GNAWED AWAY at me. I didn't sleep for days, and Relone couldn't even convince me to hunt.

"I cannot bare to see you this way."

I shook my head, looking away.

"I'm so sorry, Adam."

"What aren't you telling me?" I asked. "You spoke of love."

"I can't," he said. "It's too painful."

"We must do something. If we do not fight, The King will come after us both."

"I told you he will not hurt you."

"Are you mad?" I yelled, standing to my feet. "He burned down Elenore's house. He was intent on killing me."

Relone shook his head. "That was not Verarsoe, Adam. It was his coven—his followers."

"Wait. Why haven't you mentioned this before?"

"Because it doesn't matter."

"How can you say that?"

"Adam, it changes nothing."

I sighed. "If you don't help me, I will find him myself."

"You cannot defeat him," Relone said, his voice falling to a somber quietness. "He's too strong."

"If it is true that he would not harm me, then maybe we can reason with him."

"Reason with him how?" he demanded, his voice regaining its desperate tone.

"Perhaps we could convince him to call off his coven."

Relone shook his head again, looking away from me. "You must be mad," he said, but I could hear a smile behind his words. "And I must be mad for agreeing with you." He turned back to face me, revealing the smile.

"Is that a yes?"

He sighed. "Yes. All right. I will help you find him, but you must promise me one thing."

"What's that?"

"You must stay calm. You must under no circumstance enrage The King. He will kill you regardless of me if you insult him."

I took a deep breath, trying to calm my nerves. I wanted to do what Relone said. I really did, but I could not promise him I wouldn't lose my temper. The King murdered Elenore. How could I contain my rage?

"I know where his coven house is, but he will not be happy about me taking you to it."

"I don't care," I said. "I have to know."

"Do you remember the hotel we stayed in?"

"The one adorned with garlic and crucifixes?"

"Yes."

"Is that what was going on there?"

Relone smiled. "There are many immortal workers and spies in that hotel, Adam. Though we may be smart enough to cover our tracks, you know as well as I it's not always difficult for mortals to notice there is something…different about us—something that isn't quite right."

I nodded. "And The King?"

"His coven house is beneath." He grabbed his coat off the rack, heading for the door. "You coming?"

Chapter Two

RELONE WALKED in and didn't even make eye contact with the clerk at the counter, nor did he pay. He just walked speedily down the halls, and I followed. Nobody stopped us. He led me to a room at the end of the hall.

"No one stays in this one," he said, yanking the door open, breaking the lock in the process. "They don't even have a key for it."

We stepped inside. The room looked identical to the one we had rented before. The large bed with the floral mattress, the silk rugs, and the sitting area were all the same. Relone knelt down, lifting the rug from the floor. He pressed down with all his weight until we heard the floorboards give. He smiled up at me. "Here."

He felt around the floor and gripped something in his hand. He pulled, and the floor came up, revealing stone steps below.

"The door was hidden beneath a rug?" I whispered.

"It's better hidden than it seems."

I scoffed.

We came to an underground mansion much like Relone's catacomb, intruding on Verarsoe's evil coven. All eyes were on us; we stayed motionless until I put my hands up in a sign of peace.

"What's the meaning of this?" a gray-haired man asked. He was at least sixty when he was turned.

The creatures stood all around us, young and old.

"You know why we are here," I stated. "We demand an explanation before we burn you miserable beasts like torches!"

I felt Relone's hand on my shoulder and heard his voice in my head. *Stay calm*.

The man's eyes hardened.

"You burned the Cohen house, intending on the destruction of me—but Elenore is dead."

"You?" an older woman asked, stepping forward. "That was you? Elenore isn't dead. She can't be."

"She is," I spat. "The King himself had come to her rescue."

Perhaps that was the look of anguish I saw in his quavering face behind the flames. He knew it was too late.

She glared at me. "You commit crimes of your own as well," she growled.

"And just what sort of crimes are those?" I demanded.

"You walk among mortals, pretending to be one. You speak to mortals, befriend them. You visit theatres and churches."

"And why don't you?"

"We live beneath," she started. "We worship Satan as we are meant to."

"What is it Satan promises you?" I asked.

"He gave us our power," she yelled with a theatrical clap of her hand. "He gave us our everlasting life, our gifts —everything!"

"You really believe this? You really believe we were created to be evil? To be monsters?"

"These things that you do—that you say, they are crimes!"

"Why?" I demanded. "Why do you say this?"

"You defy the dark ways," she yelled, stepping forward. "You tell our secrets to mortals through your mind before you kill them."

"It is not as if they can expose me once they are dead," I argued.

"You live by God, do you not?" the old man asked.

"I live by neither God nor Satan," I said. "I live just as Elenore did…" I paused, and my thoughts took a rapid turn. "That's what this is about, isn't it? You did intend on Elenore's destruction, didn't you?"

"These things are high crimes!" the woman yelled.

"Why are you saying this?"

"High crimes!" she yelled. "High crimes!"

The man joined in until the entire clan was chanting "High crimes! High crimes!" and closing in around me until I thought I would be forced to cover my ears. I wouldn't let myself give in. I had to be strong. I felt the pressure of Relone's hand on my shoulder, remembering he was there, and it put me at ease.

A hush fell over the crowd, and I felt my breath explode.

The King stepped before us, his hands up in front of him. He was clad in a long robe of red velvet. Beneath the robe, he was dressed as I was dressed—white linen shirt and dark slacks. He definitely was a beautiful creature.

All eyes were on him now. He lowered his hands as the crowd fell silent. "You!" he growled, stepping toward me.

Every sense inside me was telling me to run. I inhaled, trying to find my bearings.

"You stole the heart of my Elenore. Everyone knew she was mine."

"And yet, who do you blame for her death?"

His expression hardened, and he glanced up toward the stone steps. "Go," he demanded.

The coven members scattered. They moved so fast they appeared to simply vanish. I marveled at their skill.

The King sat in a dark blue, upholstered chair and signaled me to the other. Relone stood beside me with his arms crossed in front of his chest.

"The only reason you are alive is because of your coward of a maker."

I knew he meant Relone, but neither of us corrected him.

"Who are you?" he asked in a whisper.

"Nobody," I said. "I never intended to steal Elenore from anyone. I didn't know who she was. It is not my fault she fell for me."

"I hold no anger or resentment toward you," he said.

I was taken aback for a moment. "What?"

"I came to the house to save her, but I was too late. I would have saved you too had I realized this was not your doing. I hope you can forgive me for that."

"It wasn't your doing either, was it?"

I glanced at Relone, and his expression hadn't changed.

"No," Verarsoe said. "It wasn't my doing. It was them—my followers. They were doing what they thought I wanted. Fools."

I didn't know what to say, so I remained silent.

"You know, you can move like them."

"I don't care," I retorted.

"You know you have dark powers too? You defy the dark ways, live like mortals, ignoring your vampiric nature."

Again, I didn't know what to say, so I remained silent, glancing again at Relone who was still a statue. Finally, I spoke. "I want nothing to do with your coven."

"Nor do I," he said. "How I despise them. The very thought of them makes me sick."

"Then why do you stay here?"

"These are the only beings who even care whether I exist

or not. Everyone else hates me. They loathe me, and they fear me. I cannot understand why you are not screaming at me in rage."

"Neither can I," I answered. "I feel no fury toward you. I thought I would hate you. I thought I would scream and weep and sink my teeth into your skin—I did not!"

He sighed. "Christ, how I despise them!"

He blinked suddenly, and it startled me. I shook off the shame of my so human reaction.

I didn't bother to hide my alarm when I saw we were once again surrounded by those bloodthirsty creatures.

Relone's expression had still not changed. I stood up from the chair.

The King was silent. His clan stared at him, but he did not move. They listened hard, but he did not speak.

I saw a strange fire lighting in The King's eyes—a flicker of some foreign illumination I had never before seen. He raised his hands, glancing at me. He thrust his hands down, and Relone covered my eyes.

A loud, hissing tear erupted through the crypt. Then came the screams—the loud, piercing wails of pain. I felt the fear and disgust almost suffocating me.

Relone released me, and I turned away from the burning creatures. The King led us past the torching vampires and toward the entrance. He let the coven members burn, along with most of the mansion.

Relone made hard eye contact, and I saw something in his mind—the image of a thick book with a black leather cover. I knew it must be The Book of Shadows that concerned him. If it were to be destroyed, those answers would be lost forever.

"Do not fret," Verarsoe said in response to my thoughts. "Do you think I would let that happen?"

"I cannot believe you did that!" I yelled.

"I told you," he yelled back, "I hated them. I still hate them. I want them to burn. I want them to."

I walked through the night with the pain of my loss embracing me. The cold didn't bother me. It took my focus off the pain in my heart.

I wondered about Verarsoe. He was a very complex creature. I could see a goodness in him, a goodness he would deny. After all, it was not his fault Elenore was dead, and he had destroyed those who were truly responsible.

When I arrived home, I walked down the stone steps as quietly as possible, trying not to wake my master. When I found him, he was sitting on the floor, spinning a coin. His legs were crossed, and his eyes were sad. I touched his shoulder. He sighed and shrugged my hand away.

"Adam," he started, "why so much pain?" He stood up and placed the coin in his shirt pocket. He put his hands on my shoulders, staring into me. I remained expressionless, my eyes gleaming for a moment.

"I told you," he continued. "I am all you need. You love too much. Your mortal emotions, your mortal nature—it's far too strong for your own good!"

I sighed. "How can you expect me not to care?" I asked. "How, Relone? Why? I cared for her. How could I help that?"

"I understand," he answered, and from the sincerity and sorrow in his voice, I believed him. "You loved her. I understand, but, Adam, there is nothing you can do now. Do not dwell in your misery, or you will become an empty shell of a vampire made up of nothing more than fear and torment. Do not let that be your fate."

I sighed and sat down, resting my chin in my hands.

“It will be all right,” he said, placing a gentle hand upon my shoulder. He moved my dark hair behind my ear and stroked it softly for a moment.

I turned and looked at him.

“Here,” he whispered and leaned over embracing me, letting me rest my head against his chest. “Everything will be all right,” he whispered in my ear. “You will see.”

Chapter Three

I AWOKE THE NEXT EVENING, feeling the ache of hunger in my veins. I opened my eyes but saw only darkness. I blinked over and over to clear my vision but to no avail. I could not have gone blind; that was not possible. I called to Relone. My calls were not heeded.

I heard faint voices, subtle in fragments. Thoughts. I heard my name. I called out for my master again. The voices grew louder until I could make out a few words. They were in French, which I understood perfectly. I heard talk of betrayal and crimes against the dark ways.

I wasn't at home—that I knew for sure. I felt no familiar presence. I sat up and immediately bashed my head into the ceiling, or whatever it was above me. I lifted my hand to my head and realized it had almost no room to move. I started squirming and kicking but was confined. I screamed as loudly as I could, calling out for Relone.

Please, Master. Where are you? I need you!

I was crying so hard it caused my breaths to come out in choked gasps. I tried to listen to the voices again. I understood the language, but better I understood the old-fashioned terms, styles, and order they were spoken in. I could still only make out a few words, nothing that told me what was happening to me. The terror was practically suffocating me, and I just kept screaming.

I could smell familiar scents, the smell of soil and of blood. I was in the presence of many immortals. I could feel it. I could feel hate and anger. Memories of death found their way to my mind. Their minds were completely open. I was taunted by these visions. Unfamiliar images flooded my mind. I saw The King and a lovely golden-haired woman. I felt love between them. There was affection and emotion I had never before seen Verarsoe express.

Why were these memories being sent to me? I heard more words from them—my name and Elenore's. I heard more talk of betrayal and how I must pay.

I knew who had done this to me. The name came to me slowly, and I spoke it out loud, in fact, I screamed it at the top of my lungs.

"Verarsoe!"

I didn't stop calling out for Relone, but he did not come. I was alone, trapped in a box with no way of escaping. The place fell silent. The memories of Elenore flooded back to me, bringing tears to my eyes as soon as that familiar, yet evil scent found its way to my nostrils. I gasped, screaming and pounding the top of the box with my fists. He had set fire. Verarsoe had set it on fire.

I lay there helpless. I tried to comprehend the thought of my existence ending, of truly dying. Perhaps it was better this way. Perhaps now there would be no more pain, no more loss, nothing. It would end this way, and that was all right. Just as I was finished trying to accept my fate, the lid of the box opened.

A smiling face met my eyes.

"Oh God. Relone!" I screamed. I fell into his arms.

"Come, child!" he yelled frantically. "Come now. We haven't much time."

I realized as I looked at the box on the floor of the mansion that it was a coffin, and it was on fire.

I felt no pain. I was too confused to think of anything else. Relone took me home and laid me on my bed. I lay there, reeling in pain over the blisters and shriveled skin on my legs and back from the flames. This was not over yet. Verarsoe would be back.

Relone came in to tend to me.

"You're lucky you're alive," he whispered.

"Master, how did you find me?"

"I…don't know," he answered. "It was as if my body knew where you were and took me there. I never thought about it."

"Well, thank God you did!" I said and whispered in Italian, "Grazie a dio."

"Yes," he said smiling. "Thank God."

"This isn't over, is it?"

"What do you mean?"

"Verarsoe will be back, won't he?"

"Oh, Adam," he laughed. "No, no, my young one. This was not The King's doing. It was his coven."

"His coven?" I yelled. "But his coven—I thought they were dead. I saw them burn."

He shook his head. "The ones he burned were only a fraction of those who serve him. There are others. Others who roam the world doing his bidding. He will not allow this to happen to you again."

He had said that before. "And why wouldn't he?"

"Because he loves me. He knows I will despise him if he lets any harm come to you. He will stop this vendetta. He knows of it. He's powerful. He can feel it in his blood."

I sighed. "Trahison," I whispered. "Thank you for finding me as you always do."

"Of course." He leaned over, pressing his wrist to my lips. "Drink," he said. "And heal."

"Promise me, Adam, you will never leave me."

"I can't leave you, Relone," I replied. "Life without you would be nothing but misery. I would be helpless."

He smiled warmly. "You really think you can do anything." He held my face in his cold hands. "You have such courage but so much fear."

"It is who I am."

"And that's all right," he said. "As long as you never forget what you are. Most importantly, you need to accept it."

"There is too much time left in my life. One more step and I am falling into a bottomless pit of existence."

He sighed as if he agreed with what I was saying. "Adam…" He paused. I could tell it was the start of something important to say. "It is important to make the most of the time you have. Drain life to the very last drop, and when there is no more, then there is no more. But be sure before you decide. You must be certain. Understand I was on the way to the fires of my death. I lived just long enough to find you. There was more after all, and I am glad I found that out in time."

I half smiled. "Are you ever going to tell me about The King?"

He sighed.

"You spoke of love."

"I already told you…"

"That it's too painful," I interrupted. "I know. But you have to tell me, Relone. Please."

He fell still.

"He has answers," I continued. "He can tell me the reason for all this. I know he forgives me for Elenore. He can help me."

"I cannot go with you, Adam. The last time I was there was enough pain to last me a lifetime."

"Why? What is it about Verarsoe you are so afraid of?"

"I don't know," he confessed. "But you should know my story before you leave."

"Thank you," I said kindly. I knew how much it pained him to heed my request.

He inhaled slowly before he began. "It was a very long time ago. The year thirteen forty-two. I remember it as if it were yesterday. The King believes me to be your maker. He was mine."

This was no surprise to me, but it made me smile all the same.

"I can remember always wanting to be with my master. He was all I ever had, all I ever knew.

"'Come now, my boy,' he said. 'Once you are old enough and perfect enough, I will tell you all the secrets that you wish to know.'

"Of course, I was only a young boy and understood very little. I didn't know why he was the way he was or even what he called himself. I am strong now as you know, but it took me four hundred years to become that way."

"Ancient Relone," I whispered with a smile.

"Yes." He smiled back. "My master was only home during the nights. I wept all day until he was there. I must admit I was afraid of him, his powers, his magic, and I feared more than anything becoming as he was. But of course, I was not given a choice in the matter. As much as I feared him, I loved him more than I could possibly say in any language!

"He promised me the night would come, and of course it did. It was a night of pain and fear as I remember it. He kissed me, savoring the blood he had drawn from my lips. I begged him to stop.

"'No, Master. Do not make me keep your secrets. Do not make me live like a demon.'

"But when I tasted his blood, I only wanted more. The feeling of his teeth in my neck was painful yet beautiful at the same time, so much so I didn't want him to stop.

"He broke the vein in his wrist and pressed it to my lips. You remember the feelings, Adam—the love you feel, the passion and ecstasy of the blood. I wasn't even breathing, but it didn't matter. I no longer needed to breathe. I no longer needed anything—but this.

"And then the pain came back. The pain that only our kind will ever know. No human can comprehend it.

"'Let yourself go, child. It's only mortal death. Soon, you will be strong.'

"Verarsoe told me after he turned me there were many other secrets I was to keep. He asked me to worship Lucifer as the one true master. I protested at first, telling him that Satan offers nothing but the fires of Hell. He was evil, as I did not want to be. When I refused again, he laughed. It was a beautiful, ringing, yet taunting laughter. He told me I must understand and accept that I was evil. He made me cry. I clung to his velvet, black cloak and told him I would come. I just did not want him to leave me.

"He did leave alone anyway, in the underground mansion, with the other members of his coven, called Satan's Own. Lord how I hated being alone. I didn't know where he left to or why, and to this day, I still do not know.

"That very night, a clan of ancient blood drinkers came to me and demanded things from me. They asked me where 'it' was. I swore on God and Satan I didn't know of what they spoke. I was beaten and stabbed, and I lay there on the ground. The blood flowed out of me like I had never before seen blood flow. They licked at the blood on the floor, as if trying to read my mind, as if the blood held answers—secrets, but I knew nothing.

"They demanded to know where 'the sacred relic' was, but I didn't have any knowledge of any kind of relic.

"Suddenly, a great comfort came over me when I heard the entrance open, and down the steps walked Verarsoe. I wished I could have run to his embrace, but I couldn't move. He froze for a moment, staring at those creatures, and rage boiled inside of him, his voice swelling up in his throat.

"'Get out!' he screamed. Shattering violence erupted from him, breaking all the lamps and mirrors in the room. 'Get out—out, out, out!'

"His voice frightened me, and his eyes had fire in them. He lifted his hands, and before I had time to understand what was happening, those evil creatures fled up the stone steps and out the entrance—in flames.

"Blood drew from their ears as they fled past him, out the door. They were no more than blurs to my eyes.

"Verarsoe was incredibly disturbed that night, and he placed me in a soft bed.

"'What did you tell them?' he asked coldly.

"I swore to him I had told them nothing. He asked me if my fear was causing me to lie, so he promised he wouldn't hurt me. All I possessed was fear, and I told him again.

"'Nothing, Master—I told them nothing!'

"'Just keep away from the entrance. It will remain locked. They will never hurt you again, Dark Eyes. Never again.'

"Of course, there was no great desire to know any secrets. I was too young and afraid to understand that any secret kept by Verarsoe must be incredible.

"Many times, they would return, scratching at the door and babbling nonsense. It was as if they were mindless ghosts, and all they knew was what they were after. He told me to stay away from the entrance, so I did. His fear still haunted him. The slightest sound above the door after that hotel had fallen silent, and he locked the entrance and stayed clear of it.

"I remember him feeding me the 'Healing Liquid,' which closed every wound in my body. I wondered how many centuries his blood had been distilled, purified in such a way as this. It was sweeter than the blood of a million innocent souls.

"Four years passed without the returning of the evil, but once again, they came back, scratching at the entrance. Perhaps Verarsoe was simply irritated by them. He opened the entrance, and in they fled. In an instant, he thrust his hands down, bursting them into flames.

"'Be damned to Satan's fires!'

"Again, I screamed and wept, but this time, there was little sympathy from my master.

"'Coward!' he yelled. 'For years I have protected thee. For years I have showered sympathy and love on thee, and for what? For you to lie here and cry like a child?'

"I couldn't stand the look of disappointment on my master's face. For another year, I suffered his ways and shed tears, countless on his harsh words, and harsher the tears came, harsher the words came.

"At last I did leave him, and I was alone again, waiting for the fires of my death, for my meaningless, unwanted life to end. If ever it became too unbearable—there was always the rising sun.

"I can remember that before I left, Verarsoe had told me a secret, one I was sworn on oath never to tell. Verarsoe is ancient

—this, you already know—known by others as The King. Not only is he the oldest living vampire we know of, but he is the keeper of our sacred book—The Book of Shadows. This book contains all the secrets—our power, our creation, and the mysteries of our destruction. If such a book were to fall into the hands of mortals, it could throw open the doors of darkness, revealing all our ancient secrets onto an unsuspecting world. So, it had come to this. I would carry these secrets with me, and they would die with me. Of course, it was the book the others were after, but Verarsoe keeps it safe to this day.

"I didn't want to leave. I wanted to know more, needed to understand, but I knew if I didn't leave then, I never would. I knew I would be on the ground, with nobody there to help me up, nobody there to take care of me. But I knew after that torture surpassed, I would be able to find somebody again, and I found you.

"I left him, not daring to take the book with me, even though now I wish I had. There are secrets I can share with you, secrets you must keep, that can never get out at any cost. A coward perhaps is what I was. That is who I used to be but not anymore. I am still learning though." He laughed. "After four hundred years, I am learning things from you, such as—kill the evil, not the loved."

"These secrets," I started, "are they true?"

He smiled. "Why should I lie to you, Adam? Why would I? It is a story of magic, of God, and of Satan. A story that reaches into Heaven and Hell itself. Whether these places truly exist or not, I have read these stories, and I will tell them to you in my own words."

"It was thousands of years ago. The one known as Ké Hé Zule was the first—the one who created Verarsoe. Eons ago, Ké Hé Zule wandered the earth like a vagabond, feeding on all who crossed his path. Some say he was a sinner cast out by God from all human kind and cursed with eternal life and a terrible lust for blood. No one knows for sure.

"His loneliness soon consumed him, and he created children of his own, and they created children of their own until an entire race was born. And he released into his children all his secrets and all his powers through his blood—all the gifts we now possess today. How The Father came into existence I cannot tell you. All I know is that by some force, he had been cast out of the human condition. He is the source of our kind, the maker of our maker's makers."

Though the story intrigued me, I felt more angry and let down than grateful for the knowledge. There had to be more to the story.

"That's it? So, what you're telling me is the first vampire, his source is unknown and his very existence unproven. Our source—our father is a mystery?"

"Yes," he replied calmly.

My voice fell quiet. "I don't believe a word of it."

Frustrated, I left the room, thinking to myself. A million pictures flashed through my mind. It couldn't be true, could it? Of course, if someone told me about vampires before the night on the ship, I wouldn't have believed it. My very existence proved that anything was possible. Perhaps what Relone was saying was true. But that didn't satisfy my need for knowledge. *Is everything we are still a mystery?* It was as I always feared. There were no answers. I wanted the certainty, the unchangeable proof, but there was no such thing, no way to find it. And if The Father was dead, then how? And why?

Relone came in to check on me.

"There must be more," I said.

He sat beside me on the edge of my bed. "Yes, I'm sure there is, but nobody knows the truth."

I shook my head. "Verarsoe knows. He must. He was made

by The Father. He must know something. Even something that isn't in The Book of Shadows. Something that isn't written down or cannot be written down. There is more, Relone. I know it."

"And do you really expect The King to tell you these things?"

I nodded. "I am a creature of darkness, rushing through the centuries in search of others like myself and the reason for my terrifying curse. I can only survive with answers."

"I understand," he answered. "More than you know."

Chapter Four

AS SOON AS Verarsoe caught sight of me, he saw Relone's face in my mind before I had time to block it.

"Intruder," he growled. "The only reason you are alive is because of your coward of a maker."

I decided to correct him this time. "You are mistaken on two accounts. First of all, Relone is not my maker. Second, regardless of that, he is no coward."

He laughed quietly, as if only for himself. "Oh? And you're sure of that? For he is not here, is he?" He raised his eyebrows.

I didn't respond. Anxiety started creeping in. I could feel the creature's age, see it in his face even as it remained smooth as alabaster. His features were tense, his flesh appearing as hard as marble. His black hair shone in contrast to his brown eyes that glowed auburn in the light.

"Come," he said. "I'll take you beneath."

I followed him down the steps, and it was just as I remembered it. There were beds, lamps, bookshelves…everything. It had been rebuilt so rapidly it made me uneasy.

"The door!" Verarsoe cried. He rushed past me and up the

stairs; a loud bang reverberated through the crypt. The entrance had been shut.

He sat in the blue upholstered chair I remembered, but it appeared new. He gestured for me to take the seat across from him.

"Why have you come here?" he asked.

"I need to know," I answered. "To understand, I need to know what the reason for our terrifying existence is."

"Don't let on to many others that you walk among mortals, pretending to be one."

"Why?"

"There are few vampires who do such a thing, and there are elders who wouldn't hear of it." He laughed quietly again. "You're too human."

I'd heard that too many times already.

"Why do you strengthen the ties that link you to humanity? Why not…sever them?"

I sighed. "I can't."

"You can," he pressed. "You just have to want to."

"You know what I have come for," I said.

"You want the book."

"Yes. Is there any way you would allow me to read it?"

He smiled unexpectedly. "Even if I were to let you, child—"

"Adam," I interrupted. "It's Adam."

He gave me a sideways nod. "Adam. Even if I were to let you, it would solve no mysteries and answer none of your questions. I believe it would only puzzle you more."

"I'm having trouble believing anything Relone has told me."

"Relone," he murmured. "Your coward of a maker."

"I told you Relone is not my maker."

"Then why are you with him?"

"The one who turned me left me. Relone found me and took

me in. And I would much appreciate if you would not call him a coward. You know he loves you."

His features tensed, which didn't seem possible until I saw it happen. "Relone…loves me?"

"Of course he does."

"Has my Dark Eyes come back to me?"

I didn't know how to respond, so I didn't.

"He always was the independent kind, much like you in a way. He's the one who left me. I am sure he didn't tell you that."

"He did," I confessed. "He told me many things."

"After he left me, even with my coven, I was alone," he started. "I'm surprised I haven't cast myself into the fire after these lonely, unbearable centuries."

I saw a mortal hurt in his eyes, a true glimmer of humanity. "You have something to live for now," I said. "You can help teach me. And you can bring Relone back to you. He loves you. You were his maker—his master."

"The sight of him is like a thousand different kinds of pain."

"But you love him. I can see it in your eyes."

He turned away, ignoring me. I decided not to press the issue any further and get to why I had really come.

"Can you tell me about Ké Hé Zule?"

He turned back to me, his eyes wide with shock. "The Father!" he said. "No one speaks his name aloud."

"I'm sorry. I didn't know."

"It's quite all right," he said, relaxing a bit. "Everyone thinks it. It has been a long time since I have heard his name out loud."

"Forgive me."

"What do you wish to know?"

"Everything," I said. "Where is he?"

"I don't know. I truly don't."

"Is he dead? Because if he is—"

"Impossible to tell," he said, answering my unasked question. "Perhaps he was too old. Perhaps vampires do not really live forever. Who's to say? Where is the proof we are truly immortal?"

"So, there are no answers?"

"Does it matter? I'm old, Adam. Very old. I am lonely, and I'm dying."

"Then let us save you. Or do you not wish to be saved?"

"It won't be long now before I build a fire for my flesh. I do wish to be saved, Adam. I want to be saved by you."

"What about Relone?"

"Relone cannot save me," he said. "He will never come back to me."

I fell speechless for a moment, sighed, and then spoke. "There are no children of Satan, are there?"

I saw a silent laugh shake through him. "Perhaps. For if Satan was a child of God and we are children of Satan, then aren't we all just children of God? But you have to decide what you believe in."

"I really don't know," I answered solemnly. "But as a mortal, I lived by God—"

"Lived by God you say?" His face grew hard. "You cannot now, can you? You have preyed off humans, lived off their blood. You are a creature of darkness—a monster, Adam."

I didn't reply.

"Accept what you are. It's the only way you will find peace."

"I want to know your story," I said. "I will find peace with answers."

"It is not a beautiful story, Adam. It's a tale of terror."

"That does not frighten me."

He saw the fascination in my quavering blue eyes. They flashed with wonder; I could feel it.

"I will spare you the old language if you wish."

I nodded.

"It was a long time ago, probably too long for you to comprehend. It was the year two hundred fifteen B.C. I was born and raised in France. Of course, now it is a place for tourists and museums full of broken statues. But oh, how I loved it so in those times—the vines of flowers crawling up the stone walls of my home, the snow in the winter, the smell of my mother's cooking. All of it. I wish I could have life again, Adam. I wish I could truly be."

"What you think about life means nothing to me."

"We are the outcasts of God. Cannot even walk in the daylight."

"You believe in God?"

"Perhaps. Maybe The Father was wrong. Maybe it is all false. Maybe Satan is nothing more than a metaphor of evil and it misled me."

"So why did you try to force the evil ways on Relone?" I asked. "Was it just a way for you to have control? Power?"

"You are hurt for reasons you do not understand," he said.

"Why won't you continue your story?" I asked. "Is it because you are afraid of what I will think. Is it because you still have not forgiven Relone for leaving you? You are the one who is hurt. You are the one who wants what he can't have, a religion, a companion—a life!"

No answer but sheer anger in his eyes.

"I am not Relone," I continued. "Do not speak to me as if I were. You have to suffer through this without him. You have to live through this emptiness and find what it is that compels you to continue." I stood to my feet without thinking about it. "You need to get out. Walk the streets of Boston. Why do you stay here? What is it you get out of a dark catacomb?"

His eyes flashed with fury, but I didn't back down.

"The times around us change, Verarsoe. We can too."

"What are you saying?" he mused, his anger dissipating.

"Become in touch with this age," I answered. "Find out why you are still here."

"What do I care?"

"It's a way for us to exist," I whispered. "A way for us to have life!"

"I am evil!" he said. "I live like the evil. I live beneath."

"But you don't have to."

"I choose to."

"Your story?"

"My story means nothing to you," he demanded. "You only want to know what breaks Relone's heart."

"I know what breaks his heart," I said. "You. You broke his heart. He feels you never loved him. You loved the coven who worshiped you. I do not know why your heart breaks. You can suffer this emptiness alone and find out, but until you do, I want nothing to do with you, Verarsoe—nothing!"

He stood to his feet with that familiar fire in his eyes. He turned away from me and slid his arm across a wooden shelf, sending books and lamps crashing to the floor. I instantly regretted not listening to Relone about not angering The King.

He turned back toward me, intent on hurting me regardless of Relone. I quickened my movement to the speed gift I knew I possessed. I came up behind him and sank my teeth into his neck. His blood was like every pleasure combined, everything ever loved or craved flowing into me like light—warm and welcoming.

He reached for me, hurling books into the fireplace, flailing and screaming. "Give it back! Give it back, my sacred blood!"

His rage was blinding him to where he was unaware of where I stood. He was completely mad with fury.

I ran up the stairs, out the entrance, and home to my beloved Relone.

The time passed quickly. The last time we expected to see Verarsoe in the eighteenth century, he was standing at the curb, watching in what seemed like misery as the carriage took Relone and me far away from his presence. Relone wept though he tried not to. The King stood there amidst the crowded streets, growing smaller in my teary eyes as we started onward. There were no answers now, no hope for answers. My misery was not yet over.

The carriage took Relone and me away from Boston to the smaller city of Salem. With the money I had, we could have easily afforded a mansion, but Relone insisted on stealing coffins from the city grave.

"They're dead," he told me. "They don't need them."

He knew I was miserable, but he didn't seem to care.

"I hate this," I said. "I hate you right now. You don't even care that I am miserable!"

"Why are you saying this?" he asked. "Why do you say such terrible things?"

"Because that's how I feel. I feel that if you truly love me, you will listen to me."

"You know I love you, Adam. I always have, ever since that night on the ship."

I sighed again.

"Why are you saying such hurtful things, Adam?"

I saw the pain in his eyes, and a sting of regret coursed

through me. Why had I said this to the one person I loved more than anything? Why was I always so cold?

"I'm sorry, Relone," I said softly. "I don't know why I said that. I won't be mean to you again. I don't know why I am so mean!"

"Oh, no," he answered kindly. "You're not mean."

"Yes, I am," I argued. "I know I am mean, but I don't want to be evil anymore."

"What are you saying, Adam?"

"I am mean," I continued. "But I am not proud of the way I used to live, preying off children and innocent people. I kill now only the evil. But why must I live like the devil? I don't want to do evil, so why must I live like I am evil? I want to live in a house with books, lamps, and painted walls, with beds with dark colored sheets. I don't want to live beneath the cold dirt like Satan. Don't make me threaten to leave you, for you know damn well that could never happen!"

"You are hopeless, Adam." He laughed. "I've been expecting you to say this for quite some time."

"And I have the money," I added. "Stored safely away."

"Human," he said. "Too human. You cannot pretend forever."

"I don't want to pretend I am human."

"A house? If you want to live in such a way, at least live like the amazing creature you are."

"Yes," I answered. "A mansion. A mansion would be barely what I deserve, for sometimes—I demand to be treated like the amazing, immortal beauty that I am."

He laughed. "Arrogance will be your down fall, love."

I smiled.

Soon afterward, we set out to buy a mansion, and we did—three stories, white, and very similar to the one my Rayne and I had lived in, which was still under my name. It was perfectly suited to me.

I sat on the end of my new bed and thought of Elenore and Rayne. I tried to stop it, but I couldn't, and tears built up in my eyes.

"No," I heard.

I turned to see Relone in the doorway.

"How long have you been standing there?" I asked.

"Long enough to see you weep."

"I'm not weeping," I said angrily.

He smiled. "But you want to." He sat beside me on my bed. "And that's okay, Adam." He cradled my head against his chest and held me in his arms. "That's perfectly okay. Weep. I'll still be here no matter what. And if you wish to sleep, that's okay too. I'll still be here when you wake."

I suspected he enjoyed seeing me fall weak against him, seeing my strength leaving my body. Vanity wouldn't allow me to surrender to anybody in any way my entire life. But now I lay here, crying in Relone's arms. I cried for my sweet Elenore and for her pain. I cried for Rayne, Mary, and even Madeline—all I had lost. I cried myself dry!

Chapter Five

I WALKED ALONE along the streets. The air was cold, but it didn't discomfort me. The street was quiet, which was rare for Salem. I felt lost in so many ways. The temperature dropped, chilling me for a moment, and it began to rain. I prepared to turn back and was instantly frozen in place when I saw her there, standing amidst the rain. Her eyes were rimmed with tears. The water ran gracefully over her body, and her beauty captivated me as it always had. I tried to move, but my legs wouldn't cooperate. I tried to speak, but nothing came out. The joy bubbled up inside, so I held out my arms as the only thing I could do.

She ran to me, wrapping her pale arms around my neck. I held her tightly for a long time, too far in disbelief to let go. I wanted to feel she was real, wanted to be sure I wasn't dreaming.

I pushed her forward with my hands on her shoulders, looking at her closely, her blue eyes filmed over with a crimson. I slowly leaned toward her and she to me until our lips met. Her tongue passed between my lips, and I sank my teeth. She did the same. The touch of her skin and taste of her blood held a strong sense of familiarity and desire. The pain in my heart slowly slinked away, back into the depths of my subconscious.

We stood embraced in each other's arms, the blood keeping us warm through the rain.

The kiss, the blood taunted me. How could I have ever let her go? When at last I had enough strength to, I spoke.

"You came back to me," I whispered. "Through the rain."

"Yes," she answered, touching my cheek.

My body was full of tremors and the sound of her heartbeat. The feeling left me, but I could still hear it, beating at the pace of my own. The sound faded as the taste of her left me.

"Adam," she whispered, staring into my blue eyes.

"I'm sorry, Rayne," I said. "I'm not sure what to say. I'm…"

"Shocked?"

"Yes."

"What will—what will he say?"

She meant Relone.

"The house is mine," I said. "The money is mine. There isn't much he can do outside of leaving me, which he could never do even if he tried."

"He doesn't want me," she said.

"It's not like that. He's afraid of losing me. More than anything. He's threatened by you, darling. He knows how much you mean to me."

"I have no intention of stealing you away."

I nodded. "I know."

"There's something else," she said. The urgency in her voice alarmed me.

"What do you mean?"

"I hate to confess that it was not my love that brought me back to you, Adam. I am to give you a message."

"A message from whom?"

She shook her head. "I do not know him. He found me and told me he knew I had connections to you and Relone. You must go to him and return what you have stolen, and only then would he spare your lives."

I inhaled slowly, which was completely unnecessary. Of course I knew exactly who had come to her, but I did not know how he could possibly expect me to return the blood I had stolen the night he lost his mind. It then occurred to me Relone knew something I didn't—had taken something from him.

"Adam, what is it?" Rayne pressed. "Who was this ancient creature?"

The word came to me from deep inside like something I had known my entire life. With the little breath I had left, I whispered, "Verarsoe."

"What is it?" she asked.

"Verarsoe," I whispered again, then yelled, "Verarsoe! Rayne, come with me. I must get to Relone—now!"

"Wait, Adam!" she yelled, struggling to catch up as I ran.

I didn't slow down.

"Wait! There's more. Adam, stop!"

I didn't listen. I raced down the streets until I came to my house. I opened the door, knowing Relone would be waiting for me. I put my hands up in a sign of apology or maybe surrender. "She was all alone," I said. "She has come to tell us something very important."

"Why can't you find somebody else?" Relone growled, standing up from the chair he was in, dropping his book onto the floor. "I will not let you tear apart the world we have built. I will not have it."

"Relone, you must listen," I argued.

"I must do nothing of the sort."

"It's about Verarsoe."

He froze immediately at the sound of his name. Fear slithered into his amber eyes.

Rayne stepped forward. "He said if you return to him with his sacred relic, he shall let you live. If you refuse, he will destroy you both."

I stared at Relone as realization hit me. "Damn it," I murmured. "You didn't…"

Relone stormed off to his room and returned with a heavy-looking, black book. It was closed with clasps and a lock. He handed it to me.

"Do not open this," he said.

I eyed the lock.

"Well—do not try. Take it to Verarsoe. I cannot go with you."

"Me?" I demanded. "Why me? You stole the book. How, I do not know, and I do not care to know. You're either incredibly brave or out of your mind. What did you expect would happen? What are you so afraid of?"

"You must do this, Adam!"

I sighed. "God, Relone! Is it true what he said? Are you a coward?"

"How dare you!" he yelled, pushing me back by a thrust to my chest. "How dare you insult me?"

"Then why are you so terrified?"

"You know nothing."

"I know you are scared. I know you are sending me to pay for your mistakes. Verarsoe hates me, Relone. After our last encounter—"

"You do not understand," he said. "You do not know how I've suffered."

"We all suffer, Master. Every day."

"I cannot go with you," he repeated.

I felt Rayne's hand on my shoulder, reminding me she was

there.

"We cannot delay," she said.

I glared at Relone, but his eyes were sad now. He handed me a bag. I snatched it from him, still seething with anger. I slung the bag over my shoulder.

Relone had stolen The Book of Shadows. I couldn't begin to guess how he had managed to. I also did not know how he expected to get away with it.

I wanted so badly to read it—to crush the lock into pieces until it opened. Relone told me not to, though that never stopped me before. I knew what the book held. I knew within it were more than words. There was a sort of dark energy that emanated from it, something more than I could put into words.

"Don't even think about it," Rayne answered in response to my thoughts.

"I know," I answered. "But—"

"It's dangerous," she said. "Do what Relone said. At least this once. The book is dangerous."

We took a carriage to Boston. Rayne was mumbling nonsense; she had said something about not angering Verarsoe and to be careful what you say. We stayed in Verarsoe's hotel before dawn, tucking the book safely under my pillow.

The nagging urge to read the book still tugged at me. If I were to read it, perhaps he was right about it not answering my questions. Perhaps I would not be able to comprehend it. It was also true, of course, that if I damaged it, he would punish me for that as well. I still wished to keep it, but it was not possible.

The book would go with Verarsoe and stay with him forever, and I would remain Adam Gold, the vampire with no answers, the immortal with no reason.

We did at last come to Verarsoe's hideout. We walked to the back of the hotel and knocked on the floor where the entrance was hidden. I knew he had locked the entrance, but that was no problem at all.

"Verarsoe!" I called. "Verarsoe, it's me. It's Adam. I got your message."

The entrance was opened, and Rayne and I were invited down the steps to the floor, where he sat in a chair.

"I want you more than I want the book," he started. "That's the real reason I had asked you to come here. I predict my Dark Eyes has not come along."

"You predict right," I answered.

I was nervous, afraid of him, especially considering what had happened the last two times I had been to his underground mansion.

"Why did you threaten us, Verarsoe? You would never hurt Relone. I know you wouldn't."

He sighed. "Yes, but it brought you here, didn't it?"

"Yes. I suppose it did."

"I'm dying now, Adam, and you can save me."

"No. Think about Relone. I am his, Verarsoe. I can't live as you do. I cannot be evil and regretless at the same time. You know this."

"I know what makes you happy," he argued. "I do. I can help you. I can teach you."

"Teach me?"

My vision darkened without warning, and images began to take form—visions of groups of immortals sipping blood from unseen sources, the sounds of disembodied voices in languages I did not understand. There was a sense of understanding in some of the things he was showing me—a sense of truth. I could see who I knew to be The Father. I was subtly aware of pain and despair, feelings of darkness and evil.

The images shifted, showing me peaceful, white shores and green, rolling hills under a sun that did not burn. Verarsoe, for a brief moment, allowed me to understand eternity—comprehend forever. There was something beyond the beyond that never ended. I could understand what it felt like to truly die and to be reborn again.

I didn't want the learning to stop. I wanted to know more. I wanted to know everything. I was weak now, on the floor, losing consciousness.

I forgot where I was for a time. When I came back to myself, Verarsoe was standing there, smiling at me with flashing, fierce eyes.

Rayne was crying, but Verarsoe had been holding her by the arm to keep her from rushing to my aid. When at last he released her, she ran to me, kneeling to the floor at my side.

"I'm all right," I told her. "I'm all right. Sto bené."

She hugged me to her.

"I'm not hurt," I said. "Rayne, it's all I ever wanted."

"I can give you more," Verarsoe whispered, lending out his hand. He helped lift me from the floor.

"The book," he said. "I would like my book."

"Yes," I retorted in sudden remembrance. "Of course."

I reached into the bag. No. It couldn't be. The bag was empty. *Oh, God, no.*

I turned the bag inside out. It was not possible. The thing easily weighed ten pounds. Even with my strength, I should have noticed it was not there.

"I have it," I said desperately. "Just give me a moment—if you will please."

I tried not to panic, but it was evident. I patted down my jacket. Nothing.

"Of course," I said. "Rayne, I gave the book to you, remember?"

"Adam, what are you doing?" she whispered. I knew Verarsoe had heard.

"Yes," I said. "You remember, Rayne."

I stared at The King. My fear was ice cold; I was shivering, quaking. I could feel the tremor in the atmosphere, the energy he had. The power he possessed was shaking the earth. My fingers felt frozen; my blood felt like ice through my veins.

Verarsoe's eyes were made of flames. The same fury I had seen long ago brought the same terror coursing through me. I would die this way.

The King brought his hands down.

I screamed, throwing my hands up, preparing for unexplainable agony. It never came.

There was nothing—no fire, no burning flames, no pain.

I lowered my arms, perplexed. Verarsoe stood there, not moving, as still as a marble statue. His eyes were cold and angry.

I touched him, still shaking wildly with fear. His skin was cold as ice—he was frozen!

Rayne laughed. "My God, Adam. Can it be?"

"I don't understand."

Verarsoe has the fire gift," she answered. "You can fight fire —with ice!"

"Ice," I whispered.

Grazie a dio!

The king almost drew pity from my heart. The look of fear in his eyes was so human.

He was completely aware, just unable to move. His skin looked even more like marble. It wasn't literal ice of course, but his fire clearly had no effect in his condition.

"The King?" I said to him, and then I laughed, laughed, and laughed so hard it could have become a perfect fit of hysteria. His eyes grew tenser, but he still couldn't move. I found the entire situation quite hilarious, but I had not forgotten that I had been a complete fool.

I slung the empty bag over my shoulder. How could I have been so careless? How could I have not realized the book had been lost? I had to find it now. I must.

We searched the streets of Boston and Salem for hours. The streets were damp and empty—there was nothing. We searched the hotel and carriages. Still nothing. I began to deathly fear what could have happened to the book or, worse, what would happen to me if it was not found safe.

Chapter Six

"SO, IT HAS COME TO THIS," he started coldly, his words slow and subtle. "It has spoken, thrown open the doors to the world of the undead, releasing our secrets of power and sin, where now—all can know."

"Perhaps not," I declared. "Perhaps luck will be on our side this time, sweet master, for you know if the book were to be found by a mortal, none would believe it to be true."

"Perhaps not," he answered. "It is not only the mortals who worry me. The book contains things that even many of our kind should not know. I can see your mind, Adam. You are just as terrified as I am."

"Yes," I answered, unashamed. "I am afraid."

"You do realize, don't you," he started, "that The King's power is far too strong for your gift to hold him for long."

"I do," I answered, my head bowed. "He had fire in his eyes, Relone."

"I know," he said, caressing my shoulder. "I remember the fear that paralyzed me, my body—my soul. You have courage, Adam—courage and strength. Whoever made Victor must have been old."

"Yes," I whispered.

"We have to get out!" Rayne yelled, remaking us aware of her presence. "We have to get out. Leave. Hide."

"And where do you suppose we go?" I yelled with a lift of the arms. "We have nowhere to go."

"We can find somewhere," she said gently. "You cannot face Verarsoe alone."

Relone was silent. He had tears in his eyes, his face rock hard.

"Relone?" I questioned. "Master, are you all right?"

A breath escaped his lips in a choked gasp, and he shed the tears. "No," I heard him whisper. "No."

"Rayne is right," I said. "We need to get out. I cannot do this, Relone. We must leave."

"This cannot be," he whispered. "Adam Gold, do you understand? I am his child. He knows always where I dwell. But he is not bound to *you*."

"What are you saying?"

"You must go. You must leave here soon—alone!"

"Alone?" Oh, how I hated being alone, hated it so very much. "Verarsoe would not harm those you love, would he?"

"Verarsoe doesn't care anymore," he answered. "Trust me, Adam. He would destroy you if he had the chance. My pain means nothing to him anymore. He doesn't believe I have reason to weep. 'Coward' would be the word he would use."

"I can't leave, Relon—" My voice was cut off by the sudden sting of tears. "I cannot bear to be away from you, Master. I can't!"

"You must leave here, Adam. Wherever you go, I will find you there but only when it is safe. Rayne, you are in danger as well."

"I know," she said, grasping my hand. "I shall be in danger alongside him."

"Verarsoe can find me no matter what," he said, "and if I am with you, then he will find you as well."

"So, I have no choice?"

He shook his head.

Dio mio.

"I don't think I can do this, Relone. There must be another way."

"There isn't," he said sadly. "We cannot fight The King. You know this. Even with your strength and gift, it isn't enough. Especially with his band of followers at his beck and call."

I fell into his arms, trying to engrave every detail of him into my memory.

The next night was long. It seemed as though it would never end. I was numb the entire night—worried that Verarsoe would come after us like some diabolical monster from our nightmares to destroy us all.

This was Relone's doing. For once, it was not the carelessness of the beautiful Adam Gold. It was the mistakes of the ancient Relone Akar.

Rayne was silent but very warm toward me. There were no tears in her eyes, but there were many in mine. Relone had told me not to weep, but it was something I did much of regardless.

Chapter Seven

WE WERE ON THE RUN. I had no knowledge of what Relone was doing or if Verarsoe had come looking for us. My Rayne had constant fear in her beautiful eyes of blue, and it pained me to see it.

I didn't know where we were to go; we stayed in hotels and graveyards and abandoned chapels. I thought I had learned everything there was to learn about living with the dark blood, but I soon realized things don't always go according to plan.

One night, I went out alone, walking the streets in search of fresh blood. I didn't know where I was. We moved along the way so often I had lost track. Somebody stopped me cold in my steps.

I stared at him, expressionless. He was no stranger; my body tingled everywhere with bitterness and hatred. The night on the ship rushed through my memory, making me feel almost sick.

The vampire smiled. "It's been a long time," he said.

"Let's keep it that way," I growled back.

He touched my shoulder, and I shrugged it off. He sighed heavily.

"What the hell do you want?" I asked.

"You," he replied. "I know you are alone. You need a mentor."

"You lost that right when you left me. I have found a teacher—a teacher you could never be."

"How do you know that?" he asked, arrogance in his voice but at the same time very little emotion. "You're here all alone, growing old, growing lonely. You need to be saved."

"Not by you."

"Do you know what lies through here?" he asked, pointing to a dark wood to my right.

No answer.

"A castle," he said.

"So? A castle. Leave me alone, Victor. I have nothing more to say to you."

"Go there. You'll thank me."

And with that, he was gone.

I guess I should not have been surprised he found me. I was his child after all. He always knew where to find me. Just as I could have found Madeline if I wanted.

For some strange reason, I believed Victor about the castle. Perhaps it held answers of some kind, maybe even a reason why he abandoned me.

I walked through the woods, and when I came to that castle, it did interest me. It aroused my curiosity and struck my thirst more than the blood of any human. The castle was old, Victorian, and falling apart. The shingles on the roof had rotted away, leaving gaping holes in the ceiling. Many walls seemed to have crumbled completely, and the windows were all cracked or missing. I stepped closer, seeing the floor was nothing but dirt with a few broken floorboards that were once part of well-laid flooring. It seemed enchanted, and me, as the dreamer I am, anything magical caught my attention. I thirsted for adventure, magic, and mystery. I walked slowly with wide eyes, my curiosity boiling.

I brushed my dark hair from my eyes and gazed at the old building for a long time, savoring its beauty that sent shivers through all my limbs, forcing me to smile. Why was I so enchanted? Me, a vampire, a killer—I could be walking the streets, charming innocent passersby, but instead, I stood there, staring with awe at an old, rundown castle.

I stepped inside and gasped as the boards beneath me cracked—a very human reaction to be startled so. I continued through the halls until I came to a dark bedroom. It must have been the bedroom of a child, judging by the hand-painted flowers chipping off the walls and a neglected teddy bear on a tattered mattress. A strange feeling came over me, and I shuddered; the room reeked of evil. I didn't dare go inside.

I crept along the creaking boards, nervous the entire time but not understanding why. I could hear the rats along the floors and inside the walls, even some scurrying across my feet.

I came to another room, but something about it felt different. It didn't have that dreaded scent of evil and danger. It held a sort of comfort. It was one I felt was calling to me, begging me to come inside. It was as if I could feel the presence of someone dearly loved.

There was no fear, nothing to be nervous about. I sat on the floor without meaning to and began drawing pictures of stars in the dust. I looked up and out the broken window. I gazed at the glowing moon, finding so much comfort. I wanted to stay there forever. I felt that even if the sun were to come pouring over the mountainside, I would be protected. Of course, that was not true, and I knew that, but the room was so enchanting it was free from all evil—except myself.

I looked around at the bare, stained walls, trying to find what was so inviting about it. It was mostly empty, save for an old, torn mattress against the wall. I crawled over to it and searched the area. A small crevice at the bottom of the wall caught my eye. I went over to it, but the opening was too small to see anything. I felt inclined to crack the boards around the opening, so I did. I found a stack of books. A nervous excited feeling grew in the pit of my stomach as I ran my pale fingers across them, making strange markings in the dust, which irritated me.

I blew off the dust and held them in my quavering hands; I savored the sweet perfume of the sepia paper and old ink. I opened one of the books, the cracking echoing unexpectedly through the room, but I enjoyed that sound. For a moment, I was still, listening to that ringing echo. I blew off the dust again, this time off the disconnected pages. I watched for a moment as the particles danced in the moonlight. I shuffled through the pages, but it wasn't until I came across the other book that I was interested. It was a diary. I read the first page.

17 October 1755

I told Daniel he truly doesn't understand, but he has his own beliefs, and it is hopeless to convince him otherwise. He is older and stronger than I, but yet he seems weak. He says he does not need me, that he made me out of boredom. He made me cry. I write this out of shame, but it is true. He made me cry a lot! He is gone now, and I am alone until I find another, but whom else could I want? Daniel has been mine for so long. Whom else could I want?

Victor

"Daniel?" I repeated. Chills and nervous feelings brewed inside of me. And Victor! Victor? Daniel must have been his maker.

This made me think of Relone and how he must have been feeling without me. His missing of me and my missing of him made me physically ache. I couldn't cry over him any longer.

It was a long walk, and the sun was coming, so I left the castle, being sure to take the books with me and, of course, being sure there were no others in that crevice of the wall. I walked quickly and made it home before dawn.

I climbed into bed, not disturbing Rayne beforehand. I wanted to explore the woods, wanted to so badly just to see what would happen. But I couldn't tell Rayne. She wouldn't see it the same as I did. She wouldn't see it as anything but dangerous, but I was curious, and I didn't want that to go away.

I left her a note on my bed the next evening, where I was sure she would look.

I am out. I awoke in pain. I won't be long—I ache to feed. I couldn't bear to wake you. Please be here when I get back.

Your dearest Adam

I rose at dusk; the very sun still lit the skies but not enough to harm me. I walked back to that old castle but avoided going inside. Yes, I longed for the comfort of that room but couldn't be distracted. I walked around it and through the woods. By then, it was dark and starting to get cold. I rubbed my bare arms and pulled my sleeves down but didn't roll down the cuffs of my pants, which I kept from getting damp.

I walked through the mist, and the sudden, irritating sense of déjà vu flooded my mind. I felt as if I were spinning in time, moving in and out of dimensions. I felt as if I were caught in a wrinkle or a tear in time. As I walked on, I found an area of cleared land. I continued, not afraid to let myself smile. After all—why not? Why not feed hungry curiosity?

The déjà vu was suddenly becoming unbearable, and I longed for comfort from it. This must have been a dream. If not, then perhaps I was going mad.

An uncomfortable sensation began tugging at my nerves—an alien feeling of evil, something telling me to turn back. Yet, something else was drawing me into the woods, begging me to come.

Slowly, a sound crept through the trees—music, beautiful music clearly not made by the chorus of the trees. There was someone here. I knew I was meant to follow it. Before I had even taken one more step, firm hands gripped my arms, dragging me away from the path.

"Are you insane?" Rayne demanded.

She released me in front of the castle. The change in her expression startled me. Her beauty had almost vanished. Her blue eyes were wide and tense, her features twisted into a mask of anger.

"What the hell did I do wrong?" I yelled.

Perhaps she sensed my discomfort and relaxed, looking once again like herself.

"Adam..." She let out a breathy chuckle. "You really do think you are invincible, don't you?"

"What are you talking about?"

"Adam, stay away from the woods. Stay away from this castle."

"Why?"

"You actually think I don't know you? You actually think I wouldn't find you? And if you are going to hide something from me, darling, hide it where it's out of sight."

I gasped, realizing I had forgotten to put the books back beneath the bed as I had planned. "Damn."

"You can't just go exploring the woods alone, Adam. Victor told you about this, didn't he?"

I didn't respond.

"Don't think I can't read you. When?"

"Last night," I said with a sigh. "He found me last night."

"There are people everywhere who hunt us. Be careful where you go. Be careful who you trust."

"Victor wouldn't hurt me," I said.

"I don't trust him."

I shunned her, feeling almost insulted. Victor knew I could not have resisted such a place. He knew I would find the journal. He knew exactly what he was doing, and he had gotten what he wanted from me—love. I understood him now, more than I ever had before. I knew him now, and I loved him. I realized what he truly was—a caring, sympathetic being, who lost his family and his home when he was very young and taken in by Daniel who forced the blood into him, taking away his choice. Victor did not choose the dark gift any more than I did.

I wanted to know what was making that wonderful music. It was calling to me. But I knew Rayne was right. We had to keep moving, keep running from Verarsoe and his followers.

Chapter Eight

VICTOR WANTED to draw me back to him, to bring me into his life once more. He wanted to make me love him as I once felt I did, even if it was just for that one night upon the ship. I couldn't now. I couldn't go back to him. It was time to run, and that was all I could do.

My arrogance still got the better of me from time to time. I really had much left to understand about the dark blood. Rayne was concealed inside while I left in search of food. I found my victim, a man this time. I penetrated his mind, reading his sinful thoughts of planning a murder of his adulterous wife. This was so cliché, but nonetheless, I was hungry, so he would have to do. I followed him to the street corner where he pulled out a bottle of liquor. He drank as if looking for a way to stop. He drank to the very last drop and released the bottle to the ground.

I came up behind him, sinking my teeth into his flesh. He clawed and scratched at my hands, but I barely felt it. When at last, I had my fill, I dropped him to the ground, leaning against the light post, savoring the sensation, weak all over from it.

I was pulled out of it by the feeling of unfamiliar eyes on my back. I was irritated to be bothered when trying to enjoy the pleasure of a night's kill. I turned around. A mortal man stood before me, eyes wide with fear. He held a pistol pointed directly at me.

I took a step forward.

"Back," he called, his voice quaking. "Back, vampire devil!"

I laughed out loud, throwing my head back. This would be fun.

Sweat broke out on the man's skin, and I could smell it. I could hear the racing of his heart and the chattering of his teeth. His human weakness made me almost sick. I had no desire for his blood but couldn't resist tormenting him just a little.

"One more step and I swear I'll destroy you."

I smiled again and took that one step.

"Go to Hell!" he screamed and fired the pistol three times, the sound ringing in my ears.

To my astonishment, an incredible pain filled my body, and I sank to the ground, crying out. The bullets flew through my chest, breaking the skin and pulling through the muscles. The pain of my stretched arteries was blinding. The bullets tugged at my veins. I felt as if every tendon was breaking into fragments. At last, the shots passed out my back and landed bloody upon the street.

I stood up, and the killer was still there, green eyes wide, frozen in terror. I put my hands up in front of my chest, took a few steps back, turned, and ran. I tried to quiet the clacking of my heels as I continued down the black road. Suddenly, I stopped. What the hell was I thinking? Now this man would run amuck, raving about vampires in Massachusetts. I quickened my movement to my speed gift, and before he felt me coming, I had him down with my teeth in his throat.

"Sorry, young sir," I whispered solemnly.

Okay, now to get rid of the bodies. I buried them in the

cemetery myself, making the sign of the cross as I sadly said a prayer and stood upon their graves, weeping openly. When I returned to the hotel, Rayne was sleeping soundly. I smiled. Rayne didn't need to know about this, did she? No. I could take care of myself.

It didn't take long for the running to weigh on me and my Rayne. It didn't take long to feel like life was a meaningless misery. Despite my love for Rayne, I couldn't bear it any longer.

I found myself a grave, and after I hunted for three nights, drinking enough in preparation, I chose a coffin, dug beneath the ground, and went to sleep, not knowing how many centuries I may remain there and not caring either. It was the year 1835 when I went to sleep. What awoke me I cannot say. Much time had passed, and I had no concept of how long I had been asleep, only that it had been a very long time. The world around me looked…different—the buildings, the few people out at this late hour, the odd carriages that seemed to move under their own power, shining bright light into the darkened streets. I looked down at my garments, feeling out of place but not caring much.

I stumbled along the walkways, marveling at this new time, its unfamiliar sights and foreign scents. Overwhelmed, I leaned against a large trash bin. I gasped when I caught sight of a printing—a newfangled newspaper, I presumed. My hand found my mouth when I saw it: 1987, late January. I had been asleep for over 150 years.

I came to a chapel and knelt before the altar. I knew it was time I return to my life, but there was so much missing from me, so much time I needed before I could forgive myself and accept myself. *I am Adam Gold; I am evil—and I hate it!*

I was alone in that chapel. Oh, how I hated being alone! I was loved by many, but why must my life still be miserable after all the love I am offered? Good Lord, tell me something! Give me a reason to continue, let me know you can forgive me for what I have become. Let me know that you can love me even though I am evil. I prayed, not knowing why, not knowing why I did anything.

I could taste my very own blood as tears ran down my face. I needed to feed. I was weak and hungry, and it hurt. I tried to imagine the tingling torture was God blessing my soul and the dry pulsing was him cleansing my blood from that of the evil doer. Those visions soon faded. This hurt—it bloody hurt!

I left the chapel to feed, weak and lost in my mind and my pain, slipping away from solid consciousness. I awoke once more on the alter, somewhat disoriented, my hunger satiated, my strength now returned. A vague remembrance of a fragmented memory lingered in the far corners of my mind like a dream that escaped the moment I woke, and my hand slid to the foreign weight around my neck. I removed the large, gold piece from under my shirt, admiring its beauty, oddly comforted by it.

Before I could explore the piece further, I felt his presence and slipped the medal under my shirt. I turned, meeting the gaze of the creature who was making the earth shudder. He smiled. It had been so many years, but I fell into his arms. He kissed my head.

"Ah, my Adam," he said.

I stared into his gold eyes and smiled, unable to stop myself.

"How long has it been?" I asked.

"Too long," he answered. "Can you be mine as you once were?"

I took a step back. "I was never yours," I said, a ping of grief passing through me.

"Yes," he said, lowering his gaze. "I cannot change that now. I know that. But please don't give up on me."

"I could never," I said. "There is always love between the child and the maker." I was glad to have found myself in the arms of Victor for the first time, but he was not why I awoke.

It was such a long rest without a single dream. I had become so lost and bored with life I had slept it away, and now I found myself in a new shimmering age of rock music, drugs, and parties—a world revolved around music and youth. Everywhere I went, I found people dressed in the strangest of ways and hair in unnatural colors and styles. It seemed a diabolical age, but it fascinated me and drew me even deeper back into the hands of life.

I loved the shimmering 80s. I really did. I fit right in. Being beautiful and seductive, nothing could have made me happier than living in a world where that meant so much. Though I was happy to have found myself in the presence of my maker again, there was somebody else whom I much desired to see. And when I returned to Moonlight Manor, it wasn't exactly Moonlight Manor any longer. I almost laughed when I realized…this was not the Boston I knew, and I couldn't find my mansion. Of course, that was because it was no longer standing. This would be a difficult task—to set out again in search of Relone and my beloved Rayne. It would be a hard task, but I expected to very much enjoy the adventure.

It wasn't in Boston that I found Relone nor was it in Salem. It wasn't in Massachusetts at all. I was almost angry with him for not keeping Moonlight Manor for me, but it was all right. He had kept up with my fortune and my smaller house in Salem. I found him in California, in a small apartment flat during the early evening. He sat in a chair, reading a thin paperback novel. The room was well lit and very warm looking. I loved that he wasn't resting beneath the ground in a cemetery.

I knew he sensed me, knew I was there, but I decided to have fun with it anyway. I stayed hidden for a moment and used my speed to appear in the chair in front of him. He actually jumped when he saw me. Very human. He laughingly thrust his hand to his chest, a little embarrassed, and looked at me silently. He stood up at the same time I did, and we embraced, his chest pressing the metal piece against my skin. I wept while wrapped in his arms, but it was all right. He was weeping too. I whispered "Grazie a dio" and "Thank God" so many times it became a meaningless chant.

"Is it now safe?" I whispered to Relone. "Where is Rayne?"

He sighed. I didn't like the sound of that sigh; I didn't like it at all.

"The Book of Shadows was found…many years ago."

"Isn't that a good thing?" I asked.

"No, Adam. It isn't a good thing at all."

"Why?"

"The book was found by an immortal called Joshua. He translated the book from the old French into modern English. He then took it a step further and published it, releasing it to the world in bookstores, where it could fall directly into the hands of mortals."

I couldn't respond yet. I was too horrified to say a single word. I let myself slouch down into the chair. "How do you know this?"

"Verarsoe," he answered. "Verarsoe found the creature, and through his thoughts, he found out, but death did not come to Joshua. I think The King may have other uses for him still to come."

"And the book?"

"The book…" He sighed and looked away from me for a moment, staring out the window. "Luck was on our side this time, sweet Adam," he started with a smile. "The Book of

Shadows had been placed in only a few bookstores, under the shelf titled 'Fiction,' and all of them have been burned."

"Burned?"

He nodded. "Every bookstore that carried our sacred secrets was destroyed. And all through California, immortals have been searching for any mortal with it sitting on a nightstand or a bookshelf in their warm, comfortable rooms. They take them to Verarsoe, and they are destroyed. Verarsoe's anger toward you is still lingering somewhere in him, Adam, so it would not be wise to set out to find him, but I believe he will not attempt to hurt you again. I think he has a sort of love for you, Adam."

"Of course he does." I laughed. "I like it that way."

He laughed. "Adam, you are... Lord, how I have missed you!"

I didn't respond. I wanted to say I was sorry for leaving him. I wanted to say I regretted it. I wanted to beg him to take me back again. I wanted to hold him close and let him know how much I truly loved him.

"I will take you back, Adam," he whispered. "You don't need to beg me, and you don't need to say you are sorry."

He knelt before the chair and took my hands in his, looking up at me in the kindest of ways with those tense brown eyes with their shimmer of gold.

"Stop reading my thoughts," I said with a smile. "It's rude. Besides, sometimes I don't really mean even what I think."

He gave a little private laugh and made himself comfortable in the chair opposite of me.

"But again, I must ask," I started. "Where is Rayne?"

"I...really don't know, Adam. Last I saw her was two years ago, alone."

"What?" I was stunned. "Tell me everything!"

"I was walking through Boston two years ago in...I think February. I cannot recall exactly why I was there. I wasn't looking for you. I knew that was useless, but what I did find was your Rayne. She was standing in front of a house, a large house with no lights and blue shutters. It was rundown and looked as though it had been rebuilt dozens of times."

"Blue shutters." I smiled. "That's her house, Relone—the place where I first met her when I saved her—remember?"

He smiled. "I touched her shoulder, and she turned around. I don't know why, but she embraced me for a long time. She was so sad, Adam. She missed you miserably. I didn't stay there long."

"That's it?"

"It's all right," he coaxed. "Come now. We will find your Rayne, and this time, Adam, there is no choice you will be forced to make ever again. I will take her in as I have you, and there will be no jealousy here."

I smiled. At last was all I could say to myself… At last!

We made our way to Boston through the night, and the pain of the wind made me weep, not because it hurt but because it felt so good—so good to be with my beloved Relone. When at last we reached Boston, we came to Salem to stay in my house until early the next evening. I had no idea where to start.

How long would she be able to be alone? How long until she would find someone new? I worried over these thoughts, anxious to find her.

"Where would she be, Relone?" I asked. "Does she have a home of her own?"

He almost laughed. "No, Adam. I do not believe so. Last I knew, she lived the way you used to. Do you remember the way you used to live?"

"Of course," I answered. "Moving from graveyard to graveyard, hotel to hotel, never staying in one place for more than a few nights. This will be no easy task."

"Nonsense!" He laughed. "I know just where to start."

We came to her old house, but she was not there nor was her presence. I didn't speak, only followed my master farther and farther through the city until we caught her presence clinging to the walls of an old-fashioned Bed and Breakfast.

"Here?" he asked.

"Here," I answered. "I can feel her."

We came to the top window, where we could see her sitting on the bed, alone and sad. Was she crying?

I saw a tiny hearth across from the bed and tried lighting a fire in it with my mind. It worked, and to my surprise, she sprang to her feet and turned straight toward the window where I stood upon the balcony, staring at her. Her eyes were big and red with her tears. She *was* crying. Rayne raced to the window and flung it open. She tried to smile, but she couldn't move any more. Neither could I.

"Dio mio," I whispered. Had I forgotten how beautiful she was? Had I forgotten why I made her in the first place? All of my love for her shot through me, making my actual heart ache. And just as I had done so long ago through the rain in the streets of Boston, I opened my arms as the only movement I was able to make.

She slowly stepped through the window upon the balcony and stood staring at me for a moment, and then wrapping her arms around me, she whispered over and over, "Oh God, oh God, oh God!"

It seemed Relone needed me so much more than I had ever needed him, and I liked it that way. I told Rayne about Verarsoe. Of course, she already knew, but she listened as though she had not heard it before. She listened to every word I spoke and stared at every gesture I made, savoring the long-lost essence of my presence and my love.

Chapter Nine

TWO MONTHS LATER, I sat in a little café in California, watching the breeze moving the clouds. The place was quiet when I walked in. I chose a table by myself. Of course, I would not drink coffee nor would I eat anything. The very thought made me feel sick.

I watched the mortals engaging in idle conversation. I was blessedly not hungry, so they were safe for now.

She approached me without any warning—a young woman, maybe twenty-one with lustrous auburn hair and eyes that gleamed golden.

"Who are you?" she asked, staring into my eyes.

I sensed her nervousness. "Who are *you*?"

"You shouldn't be here."

I smiled, actually amused by her thinking she had the power to make me do anything. "And just why is that?"

She sat across from me without an invitation, still staring into my eyes. She scanned the room, making sure we weren't being watched, and lowered her voice. "Because you're a vampire."

My jaw dropped, and I adjusted my collar over the chain still around my neck. I considered feigning a laugh and calling her mad. Somehow, I knew that was futile. There was nothing to make her believe otherwise.

"How do you know what I am?" I asked.

"I just do."

"How?" I pressed, forcing urgency into my voice.

She knew lying would be a very bad idea. "I don't know. I just do."

I narrowed my eyes for a moment. "Which begs the question—what are *you*?"

She sighed, lowering her head, her tawny curls falling over her shoulders. "I'm me. I just…know things sometimes. My brother and sister do too. It's just something we have…inside us."

I sat back, marveling at her, smiling.

"What?" she asked, looking away.

"You," I said. "You're an interesting creature."

"I'm not a creature."

"I didn't mean it like that."

"You should go."

"Oh, I'm not going anywhere."

I watched the color drain from her face, immediate panic spreading through her.

"I'm not going to hurt you," I said.

"You're a vampire," she retorted. "How can you say you won't hurt me?"

"Because I still possess free will," I answered.

She looked away again. "Fine." She got up to leave, but I was too intrigued to just let her walk away.

"Wait," I called.

She turned back to me.

"Sit back down, little witch."

She glared at me as she stepped toward the seat, her amber eyes tense with apprehension. "I'm not a witch."

"Well, you are something."

"I don't know what I am. And why do you care?"

"I don't know," I said. "I'm just…interested."

"Interested. In me?"

"Yes."

"Thank you, but I don't want your…interest."

"A word of advice, little witch. Don't come to vampires, making demands. That's a good way to get yourself dead."

Fear danced across her eyes.

"I meant what I said. I won't hurt you. Others may not be so kind."

"Why are you?"

"Kind?"

"Yes," she answered, taking a step closer to the seat she moved away from. "Why are you so different?"

"I don't know," I answered. "I guess I just remember what it was like to be human. I remember what it was like to feel compassion and love. It's something I've kept with me, when most of my kind choose to let it all go. It's just easier that way."

She narrowed her eyes for a moment.

"You don't believe me."

"I'm not sure."

"I want to know about you," I said, my curiosity growing.

"Why?"

"Like I said, you're a very interesting cre—person."

"I don't have answers."

"Well, perhaps you need to. I've been on a quest for answers and reason for centuries. And here I am…in a café. Things don't always make sense."

“There is one thing,” she started, sitting back down.

I could still see the fear behind her eyes. “What’s that?”

“I can let you in—in on my gifts or whatever it is my family possesses.”

I knew where she was going. “If…?”

She smirked. “If…you help me find my sister.”

“Your sister is missing?”

“Not so much *missing*,” she said. “She’s just gone. She has this fear of what we are, of what we can do. She left to ‘find herself.’”

“What makes you think I can do that? Bring her back to you?”

“Because you have the charm and you know it.”

“Don’t you have the power to do that yourself.”

She sighed again. “She’s my sister. She means the world to me. Without her…well, I guess I can say I feel a little lost. I feel weak. I don’t have the power to bring her back. I cannot help but wonder why she has such a desire to ignore what she truly knows she is.”

“I know what that’s like,” I answered softly.

“Yes, but that is because you hated what you were, am I right?”

I nodded.

“She doesn’t hate what she is.” She paused. “She’s afraid of it.”

I lifted my hands. “There you have it, chére,” I said with a smile. “Do you blame her?”

“She has never been this way about anything,” she answered with a sigh. “This just isn’t like her.”

“She’s the brave one?”

“Yes,” she answered. “Exactly.”

“So, I help you find her, and we can be…friends?”

She laughed quietly. “You want to be friends?”

I shrugged. "Why not? I'm bored, . I need something to hold my interest, and as I already stated, I will not hurt you."

She gave me a strange, accusing look. "Fine."

"I'm Adam by the way."

She stared for a moment before responding. "Ali."

It was weeks before we had any idea where Ali's sister, Maggie, was. Over that time, I had grown quite fond of Ali and her twin brother, Clement, known always as Clem.

He had very long legs regularly covered with snug-fitting blue jeans. His black hair was always slopped with gel or hair spray, and his eyes were brown. He could have passed for my mortal brother though he was very tan, and being the creature I am, I was not.

Ali's sister, Maggie, had left California, truly frightened of the things she could see and sense—the way she could see the future and speak with spirits.

Ali and Maggie hadn't been together in over a year, and Ali had never gone more than a week without having lunch or going to visit with Maggie. She was terribly worried about her and was missing her more than she ever had missed anybody.

"Please, Adam," she pleaded again. "Your promised me weeks ago, remember? If you won't do it for me, at least do it for Clem, who I know you feel a sort of love for. That you cannot deny."

I smiled, suddenly noticing her Irish accent, and it charmed me just a little. I sighed. "I found her. Just like I said I would."

Her face lit up with a smile. "Thank you!" she whispered. "So much. I promise I will find a way to repay you for this. I will tell you anything you wish to know about my family's history."

I laughed. "Just promise me you won't look at me that way anymore."

"What way?"

"With so much sadness in your gentle eyes."

She smiled, looking away from me. I loved seeing her smile. She was a very beautiful soul.

Chapter Ten

NEW YORK CITY was a beauty that night. I stared down from the hotel window at the moving traffic and people on First Avenue, clutching the large pendant beneath my shirt. I no longer cared where it came from, only that it offered me indescribable comfort. The lights sent a luminous glow upon the window, and I ached to get out again.

I watched the lights of the city flickering upon the flesh of the happy mortals. I could sense her presence within the city. Oh, yes, that was what I had come for—Maggie Hickman. I must locate her.

I found my victim early that evening, hunger overtaking me as I watched from the window. A murderer innocently passed by the people on the streets. I felt his hatred for the world and toward his father who killed his mother. I felt his grief over the hit and run that had killed his brother just a year before. I tried to penetrate deeper into his mind to move past the surface thoughts. I could see pictures of his plans, the gun in his hand, and the sweet kitten-faced girl who stood trembling in fear. This made me furious. Heat rose inside me, and my eyes literally burned with anger. I stood frozen, trying to control my rage, but it was too late. The window before me shattered, and I yelled, throwing up my arms. I sighed, my arms lowering to my sides, annoyed by my human reaction.

I riffled through my suitcase and threw on an innocent pair of loosely fitting blue jeans and a white T-shirt. I put on an old-fashioned tan colored jacket, which felt normal and good to me. I buttoned it all the way because it felt so good to be warm. Now for the hair. I picked up the bottle of hair gel and popped it open. I poured a small amount in my hand, hating the way it felt, sticky and slimy on my skin. I rubbed my hands together, cringing. I ran my hands through my hair, pulling the longer strands atop my head. Hard, gathered strands fell in front of my eyes, but at least I looked more modern now.

Although I hated to hide my beautiful eyes, and, of course, there was no sun out, I was afraid I may attract too much attention, so I put on a pair of dark-colored sunglasses. I still didn't look much different than most of the men around here.

I exited the hotel, enjoying the lights and noise of the great city. I watched my victim pushing through the crowd, looking for the perfect person to take. As I followed him, a mortal girl crossed my path. It wasn't usually like me to be distracted from a kill, but oh she was stunning. She wore a short, white skirt that exposed her pale, naked legs. Her high-heeled shoes clicked when she walked, and a white shirt hung off her shoulders and covered only half of her small breasts. She began digging through her little purse and pulled out her keys. Oh, how I wanted her. I could feel her blood in my head. The scent of her flesh met my nostrils, and I savored it. I removed my sunglasses, letting them hold up the strands of gathered hair on top of my head. Pretending as if it had happened by mistake, I ran straight into her. She let out a high-pitched yell and stumbled backward, almost falling over, her eyes big and defensive.

"I'm so sorry," I said, putting my hands up.

"It's...all right," she answered, picking up her purse and keys from the ground. She laughed. "I've been a little out of it today. You know how it is—with work and everything."

"I know exactly what you mean," I lied, putting out my hand. "Adam Gold," I said strongly, loving the sound of my own name and purposefully increasing an Italian accent.

"Katie Hunter," she answered, shaking my hand delicately. She pushed her thick, long, brown hair behind her shoulder, still smiling at me. I could read her thoughts, and she thought I was beautiful.

She was beautiful as well. Besides the perfection of her body, she had a practically perfect face. Her skin was pale and clear like that of porcelain, and she had large, round, brown eyes and delicate pink lips. She was very innocent looking.

"What kind of accent is that?" she started. "If you don't mind me asking."

"Italian," I said, satisfied she had noticed.

"Oh, don't be embarrassed," she rejected, putting her hands up. "It's beautiful."

"I'm glad you think so. Io reconoscente."

"Where do you live?" she asked.

"Just visiting."

She was speaking again, but I couldn't hear her. All I could hear was the loud pounding of her heartbeat. Didn't she notice my skin was a glowing white, my eyes fierce and cold? What about my teeth? Why didn't she notice my fangs even when I wanted her to?

Her heartbeat grew louder, pounding like a bass drum, a perfect mortal rhythm. I could physically feel my blood in my limbs; I could hear it rushing through me like the sound of a flowing river. She didn't deserve to die this way—not in my arms. But it was too strong, the taste of her life in my mouth.

I took a step closer. There was no need for my other victim.

I wanted the beautiful Katie Hunter, the innocent soul. I had forgotten completely about the bastard murderer I had been following all night as I took Katie by the waist and sank my teeth. Her blood was hot and spicy on my tongue, and it burned all the way down. Such beauty in killing, such ecstasy in feeding. I stepped back, and guilt came immediately.

"Dio mio," I whispered. How could I yet again? "Sorry, darling," I whispered. "Truly I am." I took her purse and returned to the hotel within seconds. Thankfully, nobody had seen. After all, people get mugged in New York City every day.

I sat at the small table and rested my forehead in my hands. It wasn't enough just to weep. *I am a vampire, a killer, and to weep would do nothing but pain me more. This is what I do. I hunt. I kill. I feed. This is what I am.*

I needed to find Maggie. That was what I was here for, and I had felt her presence but ignored it, delayed. I decided it was time. I found my first victim, the murderer I had been stalking, and I took him down. There was little satisfaction, no sport at all. Ah well, better than an innocent like Katie.

I found Maggie in a café that was surprisingly quiet. She was sitting alone, her red hair up in a small bun. She stared into the black coffee on the table before her, but she didn't drink it. She sensed me as I expected.

She looked up from her coffee, and her golden eyes locked on me. I smiled. She jumped up from the table, but before she had time to move a single step, I stood right before her. She jumped back, thrusting her hand to her chest.

"Please," I started, raising my hands. "I mean you no harm. My name is Adam." I didn't want her to be frightened of me.

"I know who you are," she said, "and I know my sister wants me."

"Ah, so you can read my thoughts."

"I guess you could put it that way."

"Don't be frightened," I soothed. "I mean you no harm. I swear it."

"You're a vampire," she argued. "What do you mean you don't wish to harm me?"

"Say it a little louder next time, chére," I said with a smile.

"Please just leave me alone. Please!"

"Your family needs you. Your sister is miserable without you, and your brother loves you more than life."

"They don't need me. They are…well, I don't know exactly what to call them."

"Witches?"

She ignored. "My point is I have come here to find myself. I know it may sound like a cliché, but I want to know who I am, and until I do, nobody else can."

"I can," I whispered.

"How is that possible?"

I hadn't realized she had heard that.

"I have good hearing," she mumbled.

"I can read you, darling. You are a witch. What's so wrong about it?"

"I am not a witch!" she demanded harshly.

"You're gifted, ma chére. You and I both know that."

"So—what's your point, Mr. Arrogance?"

I laughed. "No need to get angry and sarcastic. My point is…you already know who you are, and you're afraid of it, so you have come here to change it. But you can't, darling. You can't."

"It's Maggie," she whispered.

"I know your name. You need to come back. Your family misses you. What is so terrible about returning to California where you belong?"

"I wish to stay here."

"No, you don't." I laughed. "Come. I can take you with me."

She took a step back.

"You can come along by choice, or I will drag you with me."

I sensed her panic but didn't care anymore if she was frightened. "Come now. I'm taking you home!"

She took another step back. "This is not your concern!"

"But it is," I argued. "I will drag you kicking and screaming if I have to."

She must have known fighting me was futile, so she finally agreed.

I knew as soon as he walked in the door, without even looking. It was my beloved Clem. He smiled when I turned to him, dark brown hair messy and sloppy upon his head. His eyes were big and round. He was in his early twenties, perhaps older, but his face was childlike, showing very little age. He said once that as soon as his eyes met mine, the word "vampire" was whispered in his ear by some "unknown force."

"You've come," I said.

He smiled, and I removed the dark sunglasses from my eyes.

"Of course," he answered. "I will always come when you call, and I am always here when you need my help."

"Need your help? Who told you that?"

Through the messy strands of my black hair, I could still see the tremble in his eyes, and I couldn't help but smile.

He smiled sarcastically. "Come on, Mr. I can do anything all by myself."

I laughed. "I called you here to let you know that… Well, look for yourself."

He gave me a perplexed look.

"In the other room," I said. "Go look."

I followed him into the other room, and as soon as he saw his beautiful, red-haired sister asleep in the bed, he smiled and embraced me.

"Thank you," he said. "We were so worried about her!"

"You should let her know that."

"Let's not wake her yet. How on earth did you get her here?" he asked. "As stubborn as she is…?"

"I have my ways." I laughed. "As always."

The next evening, Maggie left Relone's apartment and went home to her own tiny house after letting Ali know she was well.

"My God." Relone laughed. "Adam the magician. You really can do anything."

I laughed. "No. I am only Adam Gold."

Chapter Eleven

AFTER SETTING up the deed and property for my new manor to be built, I felt the need to get out. I needed to smell the air again and feel like the old Adam. I was sensing a kind of strange anxiety in my gut. I took a walk through the dark streets of California but wasn't hungry; I was too busy enjoying the night in itself.

I continued down the streets with my hands in my pockets, staring at the ground. I didn't feel like myself. Depression was setting in again, and I couldn't figure out why. Some strange foreboding was clinging to me. I tried to ignore it and enjoy the serenity of the nighttime. A lot of evil caught my senses that night, and I wished I was aching to feed, but I couldn't. I had no appetite for the sport or the blood. I sighed and decided to turn back and head home to Relone's place. I was growing impatient for Moonlight Manor to be finished.

I was distracted by an eerie sound, almost piercing through me. It was the sound of music. It was very much the music I had heard that night in the woods near Victor's castle in Boston. It was miraculous. It was a choir of life—like the sound of a million different heartbeats and a jumble of thoughts and feelings. It was a force of energy unlike anything possible to duplicate. I followed it through the darkness and came to a secluded area of trees and rocks. It was a lot like the woodland I was drawn to back in Boston. I couldn't decide if what I was feeling was real or simply my imagination, but the feeling in my gut rose to the top of my head, and the déjà vu expanded erratically and rapidly. I pulled the piece from my shirt, gripping it tightly as it all returned to me. I gasped for breath, which was a very human thing to do, and I realized it. I continued walking as if my body was moving without my mind. I wasn't thinking about anything but how to rid myself of these feelings and this thirsting curiosity.

He looked at me in an unnatural way for a moment.

"What are you saying, Clem?" I asked.

"Verarsoe said something about talk of war."

"You spoke with Verarsoe?"

He nodded. "I went with Relone."

I sighed. "I didn't want you to have to know these things, Clement. You are mortal and delicate. Do you remember when I told you about that music I heard in Boston near Victor's old castle?"

"Yes."

"I heard that music again, Clem. That's when all of this happened. In my weakened state, it must have affected my mind. I didn't even remember. It wasn't until earlier today I even knew the name, but it all came back to me."

"Name?"

I nodded. "It was just after I awakened. I was weak and hungry. That music I heard back in Boston was a clue—a warning almost. I heard it again, but this time, she came to me —spoke to me."

"Adam, what are you saying? Verarsoe seems frightened, as if you are the only one who can change what will happen."

"I am. I am the only one. She found me for a reason."

"Who?"

I sighed, turning away, almost frightened to speak the name out loud. "Sekhmet," I whispered.

He stared open mouthed. "The lover of Ké Hé Zule," he replied, almost breathless.

"Yes," I answered. "She wants me for something. I am unsure what, but she has evil plans of something, Clem. Whatever she plans on doing…" I sighed, breaking off. "All who agree will wish to help her, and their young ones will follow. All who oppose will have followers as well. Not only will this cause a war, it could scatter our secrets across the globe!"

He sighed. "What did she say to you?"

"A lot of things. Meet me here tomorrow night. Relone has called together a meeting of some sort. I can tell you the whole story then."

He nodded. "You always have a way of fixing things, Adam."

"Yes," I whispered. "But I am afraid this is a bit beyond fixable, Clem. This is a disaster beyond anything imaginable."

"You're telling me this?"

"Why lie to you? You would know anyway. You have mind gifts the same as my own."

He nodded. "You have a strange way about you, Adam. Things I'd rather you didn't tell me, you speak of without caution, and then when I beg you to explain things to me, you say how you wish to not burden me with your worries."

"I am strange, Clem?"

"I didn't mean that, Adam."

I chuckled. “No. I took no offense. It is who I am.”

The meeting the next night was awkward. They were all looking through me as if my mind were open and they could simply read my thoughts. This had to be done properly. I would tell them all word for word exactly what had gone on that night. It was a fateful night in many ways.

I had done it again—unleashed things I couldn’t control. I had to tell them now as they stared at me that awkward, frightened way.

I felt the pressure of Relone’s hand on my arm, and it comforted me, making me a little less nervous to begin.

Clem was staring at me as though he couldn’t hope to understand what I was about to tell him. I smiled at him, or I tried to. I took a deep breath and began.

“I don’t remember how it first came to be that she had found me,” I started. “It was a night like any other, only this time…I heard music—music as I had only heard once before a very long time ago in the woods near Victor’s old castle in Boston. I was so enchanted by it that I followed the sound, trying to find where it was coming from. It was as if the stars were speaking to me. I cannot any better describe the beauty of this music. It was made by some inhuman force. It was more of an essence emanating by some intense power.

“Before I realized how long I had been walking, it became very dark, and I, even with my vampire eyes, couldn’t see anything but blackness. I was terrified, whimpering, and running around. I began bumping into things and calling out for Relone—but he didn’t come. My vision went red with confusion, but I refused to lose consciousness. I tried to calm myself.

“*It’s a dream,* I thought. *It’s only a dream.*

"The music grew louder, more intense. I continued to run into things, not being able to understand why I couldn't see. I knelt down, trying to figure out what kind of ground I stood upon. It felt like marble, cool and smooth, so I let myself lie down, where I would not sleep. I started to cry again, and closing my eyes, I began whimpering the name of Master, but still, I was alone.

"Finally, my eyes opened, and shapes came into view. Only white shapes at first, but slowly they began to take form and gain color, and I saw where I was—a room with a marble floor, white like the snow, with fine lines of black swirls. Golden upholstered chairs, golden curtains, and a golden rug. It was a room fit for a king. I smiled, suddenly forgetting all of my fear though there was still confusion.

"I saw her face. Deep, golden eyes stared hard as if they could be fixed on me forever. Black, silken waves of hair dark as the night fell delicately upon her small breasts. Golden strands of beads were woven into her hair, so she truly looked like a princess. And she was. She was a princess.

"She spoke to me. Slowly and precisely.

"'What you see is only an illusion. What you feel is an illusion.'

"Her voice was not unnatural, but it had a faint ring of age to it that echoed through the room, sending chills through my body. I sat up, and she took my hand.

"'Adam Gold, I know who you are. And you know who I am as well. No words need to be spoken.' I realized then her lips hadn't moved.

"'Rise up, my prince,' she whispered. 'Rise up.'

"I stood to my feet. I cannot tell you what happened next, only that she fed me her blood. All I remember is being back in that chapel, knelt before the alter, thinking I had been dreaming. She had left me with something—something to remind me it was not a dream. She had placed a medallion around my neck, a metal medallion with the letter 'S' inscribed on it. It was formed by strange hobgoblin-looking creatures, each touching one another, connecting the form of the letter.

"She is coming back for me, coming back to fulfill her devious plans. What exactly those plans are I cannot tell you. I do not know, but she is moving. She is on her way. There isn't much time left!"

For a long time, they just stared at me.

"You must destroy the medallion!" Relone declared.

"No!" I yelled back. "She can find me without it. She found me the first time, didn't she? With it, I can sense when she is near, and I can be prepared. If I cast it away, I will be clueless as to when she plans to strike next!"

He sighed. "Good Lord."

"Sekhmet is waiting!"

Chapter Twelve

HIS BROWN EYES were tense and focused hard on me.

"You told me Verarsoe had a message for me, Clem. You never told me what it was."

He was silent, staring off as if in a deep state of thought.

"Clem?"

Startled, he focused his eyes on me. "I'm sorry. I'm still in a state of complete disbelief. Your story was…incredible, Adam. What were you saying?"

"Verarsoe's message. What was it?"

"Of course," he said, shaking his head a bit as if to clear his mind. "He said something about war, but he also told me something about The Book of Shadows."

"The Book of Shadows? What can the book do to help us? She will snatch me up again. She will do something terrible. She has evil in her blood, Clement Hickman. She is too powerful for the book to do us any good."

"But there may be a way to stop her."

I listened to the glimmering Irish accent breaking through his words.

"There are elders the Book of Shadows mentions, one…by the name of Lacara."

A sudden spark of hope came over me, and I smiled, but it was a fearful smile, and he knew it.

"I don't like when you look at me that way, Adam."

"What way?"

"With so much fear behind your eyes."

"You can see that?"

"How could I not?"

I sighed. "I look at you that way, Clem, because I cannot hide my fear, and what is vanity now?"

He nodded. "Don't ever feel weak, Adam Gold."

"I don't. Just foolish sometimes—and evil."

He shook his head. "You're hopeless."

"So, Lacara?" I stared. My eyes moved across the warmth of his skin, his pinkened lips, and cheeks, but I had no desire for his blood. At least…not right now. "Where can I find her? Clem, you must tell me!"

He laughed quietly. I found no humor in this situation at all.

"You really do think you can do anything, don't you?"

I smiled. "No. I am just Adam Gold, but I do have some strength in me, Clem. Now tell me where she is so I can find her!"

Clem's eyes flashed. "I thank you for doing this. For taking it upon yourself to save so many. You are truly a creature full of goodness. You are not selfish at all!"

I shrugged him off, but he only smiled at me.

"The Book of Shadows mentioned her only in poems we cannot understand," he continued. "Not even Verarsoe can understand them. The only ones who can are the ones who wrote them, so I cannot tell you where to find her."

"But I will, Clem," I answered. "Because I must!"

I sat back in the chair, thinking about Rayne, and then came the thought of The Mother. I knew I had to do something, but what I had to do frightened me.

Clem was a beautiful person, one that if he were to become one of us, he would still have a lot of humanity left in him. Sekhmet had taken a lot of mine by feeding me her blood. Of course, I was still Adam Gold, just more potent than ever before, and that was just fine with me.

The queen knew no limitations, and I thought on this, wondering what other kinds of powers she had given me. I knew I would begin to weep if I sat there long enough in search of a reason. I had to stop myself, so I stood up and walked around in the warm room for a few moments, trying to clear my head.

"This will not be easy!" Clem announced.

"Oh, I am not expecting it to be," I answered. "I am just hoping Lacara can make all of this a bit easier on me. She will, won't she?"

I realized Victor had entered the room. I didn't know Clem had called for him as well.

"Of course she will," he answered. "But, Adam—you are not invincible!"

"I wish everybody would stop saying that," I demanded, sighing a little. "I don't think I'm a god. I don't want to be. I am Adam Gold. Adam Gold will save us. Adam Gold will win."

Victor sighed. "I'm sorry. I fear for you, my son. I love you. You know this. Relone loves you too. I came to him once, and he told me his story—which he is putting in writing as we speak. He loves you, Adam. We all do."

I sighed again. "So what do you propose I do?"

"Just be careful," he answered. "Please."

I nodded my head. "Si tesora."

I was surprised at Victor's calmness about everything, his emotionless attitude. I embraced him, and he kissed my forehead. I looked to Clem, just behind my Victor, standing at the door.

"Come on now," Clem said. "You won't be alone this time, Adam. As I promised."

I smiled faintly, trying to show some comfort through my fear of this journey I really didn't want to take. I didn't want to be alone, but I worried about Clem so much. I wanted to just say, *Andare a casa, Clem.* I just wanted him to go home—to be safe! But I knew he wouldn't no matter how much I begged, and I wasn't sure I really wanted to.

"You're the one who knows about Lacara," I started as we continued down the streets. "Where could she possibly be?"

"I really cannot tell you," he answered. "Sekhmet gave you a power to see things, didn't she—through her powerful blood?"

"Well, yes, but…"

"Use the medallion," he said softly with a fair, somewhat arrogant smile.

I smiled and shook my head. Of course. I gripped it in my hand, and a rush of visions came to me. It was a dusty city, artificial and full of white stone and statues. There were beautiful fountains and green vines crawling up the walls and onto the balconies of the little houses. There were lovely, dark-haired mortals with russet skin. It was warm; I could almost feel the heat of the sun, which I had not felt in centuries. This city was ancient and full of tourists, but why was I seeing this during the day? Is this what I had asked for?

Night!

The city darkened, the people vanished, and the moon glowed. I smiled and sighed in the comfort of my nighttime. There were no people around the streets, and I saw myself in these visions, sneaking into the little houses and stirring my victims from their nightly beds and feeding cruelly. Aw, yes—

making me hungry! How different I must look to them! My white skin and glowing blue eyes.

I could not describe these visions perfectly, of course. Some parts were very fuzzy. But I knew the city, and it came to me like something I had always known like a long-forgotten dream.

I came back to myself and released the medallion. I smiled at Clem and whispered. “Rome!”

“Italy.”

“Yes,” I answered.

We smiled.

“I have no sense of the direction of Italy,” he said.

“Neither do I,” I answered, bowing my head a little, as to look straight into his eyes, and I smiled. “Come on now. This may be uncomfortable. Keep your eyes closed.”

I remembered the way Victor had raised me from the floor of the ship all those years ago. I knew I could do the same. With this new potency, it was just something I felt inside me.

I grasped his wrist and rose from the ground. Clem yelled and clung to my shoulders. I guessed he had never done this before, never even known about it. “You’re not going to fall,” I said softly. “Don’t worry.”

He was shivering, and the fear emanated from him, coursing through me.

“Believe,” I said.

I closed my eyes and grasped the medallion, asking for Rome until my body took me where it knew it needed to go. Clem kept his eyes shut, and I instructed, fearing the stinging pain of the wind.

His fear was greater than mine was when I was alone up here with Sekhmet, and her beauty alone frightened me. Alas—he was afraid to die! Maybe now he would be my child after our little saga was completed.

Chapter Thirteen

WE ARRIVED NEAR DAWN. The city was marvelous, absolutely magnificent, but the sun was coming, and I needed to conceal myself from the light.

I found a hotel, and we rested there. When I rose, the streets were silent, and the air was still warm. The moon was unbelievably bright. It was a beautiful city, made by the hands of man.

We set out without delay in search of the elder. We looked around the streets, and nowhere did I feel a presence clinging to the walls of a building or lingering on a street corner. We searched for hours to no avail.

"I think Verarsoe is just as frightened about all of this as we are," Clem said. "He wouldn't have told me unless he was sure we could find her."

"Si tesora," I whispered. "Si tesora."

Just when we were about to give up hope in finding Lacara —she found us.

I turned around and stared, frozen, unable to think or move. She was breathtaking. Golden hair in crimped waves shone like ribbons in the moonlight. Her smooth, alabaster skin was perfect like that of a doll. Her eyes were dark blue like my own, gleaming as they gathered the light. I could feel the age in her, the tremor in the atmosphere so much stronger than Relone.

The woman smiled, and I lost my breath completely. Her beauty was literally breathtaking. I was unaware even of Clem, who stood right beside me. Her power struck me almost like pain through my limbs. I knew she could read my thoughts, and I didn't care. Whatever she was seeing within my head made her smile.

She didn't speak yet, just stared as if waiting for something. I remembered Clem when I felt him clutch my shoulder for support. If I hadn't been there, he probably would have fallen. I opened my mouth to speak, but she put her fingers to her lips to silence me. I probably wouldn't have been able to speak anyway; I hadn't any air left in me.

She held out her hand delicately. I wasn't exactly sure what she wanted me to do, and her beauty confused me. I took her hand. There was a look of approval in her eyes, and I smiled at Clem. She glanced at him, signaling him to follow.

She led us only a few feet away, out of the moonlight and into the darkness without speaking a word.

Clem clutched my shoulder again, and I touched his hand.

"Adam…" he whispered, and his air was cut off.

At last she spoke. Her voice was dark, but a ring of age in it trailed through me, making me shudder. "The only name you will ever be able to speak is Lacara," she said.

I pondered for a moment—the difference between the names. Her real name, which she told me through her thoughts, was impossible to speak out loud. It was Lacara with silver syllables between the letters. I shuddered.

"Of course I know of your search for me and my sisters," she started. "The others are just as I am, so do not be expecting relief from confusion because you will not find it. You cannot yet understand our age—the centuries we have lived." She paused, making eye contact with me and giving me a slight half smile. I didn't know what it meant.

"And you, Adam Gold, with your search for goodness and lust for evil. You come all this way to meet creatures of such age and power to save creatures you believe should never have come into existence to begin with?"

"I have," I answered. "I do believe that, but the fact is, we are here. We do exist. And Sekhmet's plans will start a terrible, gruesome war!"

Clem sighed as Lacara turned away, and he touched my shoulder. He wiped the sweat from his forehead with the back of his hand. His entire body was trembling.

He didn't want her to speak to him. She frightened him even more than she frightened me. She seemed to enjoy it.

"So, you wish for me to help you?" she asked.

"Yes," I answered. "This will mean the destruction of so many. Please. I mean no one any harm. I have no intention of going with her."

She turned to me slowly. "I know," she whispered. "But you will."

I couldn't answer.

"Adam, you will come with me, and Clem, my sisters will take you. I must have my time with Adam."

Before I realized it, Clem was being led off by three other beautiful women, who smiled at him and fondled his hair, making him weep silently.

"Why do you fear so much?" she asked. "This is not your doing. I can see your mind. You have power, Adam. You are loved by all. Why do you think Verarsoe spared you? Why do you think Sekhmet has chosen you? You were chosen to lead the new era."

"Not to stop a war," I said. "You have that power."

She smiled and slowly leaned in, meeting my lips with hers.

Her skin was soft and warm. It felt so human that it baffled me even further.

I couldn't speak for a moment, paralyzed by the ecstasy of her touch.

"I need your help," I said when I could finally speak.

She leaned in again, and once more, our lips met. The pleasure was maddening. I didn't want it to stop, and how could I resist her?

"Lacara, I—"

"You do not need to speak," she told me softly. "You can stay within my protection, here in this beautiful city."

"I can't, Lacara. I came here to ask your help, not your protection"

"There is not much I can do, Adam."

"But you can try."

"Yes," she answered. "I can, but I won't. This is not my concern. You are mine now, Adam. Don't you want to be?"

I couldn't answer. I couldn't say no.

She brought me to her home and into a beautiful little room, very modernized, which clashed with the ancient buildings around it, but it was comfortable. She loved the mortal ways too; she understood the separation between good and evil.

She had a bed, lamps, and books by the hundreds. So many books! She sat beside me on the side of the bed.

"My Adam, why do you fear?" she whispered.

"You can't do this, ma chére. Please—I need your help."

"And why is it my place?" she snapped. "Why should I be the one to save our kind from their own mistakes. This is not our concern!"

"Even you cannot fight Sekhmet," I said. "When she comes for me, you will not be able to protect me."

She kissed me again and again, and I kissed her right back, not being able to stop myself. I had forgotten how much I loved

Rayne. I had forgotten how much I missed Relone and Victor. I had even forgotten completely about Clem.

I didn't know how the time passed. I couldn't remember anything except Lacara beside me every minute, clinging to me and kissing me—always loving. Why did she love me so much? What had I done? All she did was look at me and read my contradictory thoughts.

I wondered how Clem was doing, what was going on with him and Lacara's sisters. Of course, I had begged Lacara over and over to release me, but she lavished affection on me and brought me to her so I could not escape. Sometimes I felt as though I was going mad with confusion, screaming nonsensical phrases in Italian until she could calm me.

I fed off her viciously and she off me. I knew I shouldn't have, but how could I have turned away from her? Her beauty captured me and held me as if I were a prisoner of her love.

I felt as if I were inside a dream, trying to stop slipping into these stages of unconsciousness. I tried to look at my surroundings, to focus and to feel awake, but my conscious mind kept falling asleep. I locked my eyes onto a stained-glass lamp on the nightstand beside the bed. I tried for a long time to not take my eyes off it. I tried to trace the designs in the lamp and understand what the shapes were—trying so hard to feel conscious and alive. She entered the room and ran her fingers across my hand, pulling it away from the lamp.

"No…" I whispered. "I have to stay awake. I have—I have to…"

I tried reaching for the lamp, but she was too strong. She softly ran her hands across my face and my arms. "I need the lamp," I said. "I need to stay alive." I was on the very verge of madness.

In a matter of seconds, I had completely forgotten about the lamp and had my teeth in her throat. She let her head fall back, and her breathing quicken as I drew her powerful blood from her body. She moved away from me. My mouth formed words, and the blood dripped from my lips onto my hand as I tried to speak. I wanted more.

She began to unbutton my shirt—the mortal way, slow and almost clumsy. She slid the fabric off my shoulders and across my arms. I inhaled a gasp of breath. I was shivering now but not because I was cold. I was unsure why I was shivering, but I was comforted by her hands on my chest.

She touched in a strange way—like a mortal would have, examining the hardness and loving the feel of my skin. It was absolutely maddening. She pressed her lips to my chest and began kissing me before biting. She used her teeth as a soft caress, so soft I almost couldn't feel it. She bit through, and I gasped. I let out a moan, and she pulled away.

"Did I hurt you, Adam?" she whispered in my ear.

I couldn't answer right away. All I could say was, "Please don't leave me."

She smiled and returned to the wound on my chest. There was no pain, and I was sure she knew. She didn't stop until I began to feel sleepy. When she pulled away, I realized what had just happened. My mind woke up, and my thoughts were racing. *Why do I not consciously understand what is going on? Why am I so detached from reality?*

Finally, I slept but not for long. I awoke again, and this time, she didn't even kiss me before shoving me against the headboard of the bed and sinking her teeth into my chest. I moaned again from surprise and pleasure. Why me? I tried asking myself things. I tried to think of things. I didn't feel awake again because I couldn't remember anything. I knew there were other people besides me and her—there were other creatures whom I loved—but I couldn't remember a single one of them. I couldn't even try to remember because I was distracted by her love.

I let myself go then; I let my mind fall asleep. I couldn't fight any longer. I closed my eyes and took in the kiss she gave to me.

All I remembered after that was staring mesmerized at the shimmer in her bare skin, the perfection of her beauty. I fed from her viciously. I couldn't control myself. I was like a lion attacking its prey. She let me lose myself in her presence. She let me bite into her without compassion. I bit deeply not only for the blood but simply for the pleasure of feeling her perfect skin in my teeth. I was possessed by passion and imprisoned by pleasure.

I wept, probably because of the things she was telling me—things about The Book of Shadows, the poems and writing she was letting me understand. She loved me without me having to speak a single word. I couldn't help that I was desired; I couldn't make her stop wanting me.

As the days passed, Lacara's affection seemed to be waning, and I was the one bringing her to me. I couldn't understand why she didn't want to be close to me anymore, why she didn't want to feed off of me as we had done before.

I awoke one evening to see her awake, sitting up on the side of her bed, refusing to turn to me. I touched her shoulder, and when she turned around, I gasped to see she was crying.

"My darling," I whispered. "What reason for tears now?" I leaned forward, but she refused to kiss me.

"We need to leave here," she said. "Tonight—now!"

"What?"

"We need to leave here," she repeated. "We need to return to California. This war must be stopped!"

"Why do you say this now? Why so suddenly have you changed your mind?"

"Adam, listen to me," she started strongly. "Do you not feel the power I have over you? Do you not realize you are only free when I release you? I do not want it that way, my love—I truly don't!"

I had no memory yet of Relone, Victor, Rayne, or Clem until she spoke again.

"Sekhmet is moving," she said. "She is preceding the madness. I can feel it. Listen to me, Adam. Don't you remember? Sekhmet and The Book of Shadows? The Father?"

A flood of memories came back to me, crowding my mind. I felt that dreamy sensation of the past, and suddenly my soul filled with tortured worry. Time was running out, and now we must go. We must save them. We must fetch Clement Hickman and depart tonight!

Chapter Fourteen

"HOW CAN we stop her when she snatches me up again?" I asked. "I don't know if I can do this. Dio mio!"

"That is why I am here," she answered. "Perhaps with my power, we may have what it takes to bring her down."

I sighed. "You're right then. We do need to leave tonight. Will your sisters be joining us?"

"No," she whispered as if she thought I couldn't hear her. "Come with me. We are going to get Clement."

She led me off to where her sisters sat in the place Lacara and I had first met. They were sitting on the white stone of the fountain.

Lacara approached her sisters as they hung all about Clem, gripping his arms and kissing him. He looked as though he had been crying for days. His eyes were red and puffy, but his gaze was far away—half asleep and dazed as I had been.

Their eyes all met Lacara's. One of them embraced her, weeping and glancing back at Clem. No words at all had been spoken, and I couldn't hear their thoughts. Lacara nodded at her. Even though this woman was weeping, she was still magnificent. She had medium brown hair that reached her waist, thick and full. Her eyes were brown too, but she had very little coloring in her cheeks and lips. She was probably hungry.

Lacara pulled Clem from their grasp. They clung to him still, letting him gently slide from their silken hands, and they all wept in each other's arms. The brown-eyed girl approached him as he stood beside me. I had guessed she wanted to say goodbye. She touched his hair with her fingers and placed her hand behind his head, pulling him closer to her. She smiled and kissed him. He opened his eyes slowly as she pulled away, and he stared at her, crying again. He glanced at me and kept his red, swollen eyes locked on me for a moment. I smiled at him, and he fainted in my arms. I silently laughed, tilted my head at Lacara's weeping sisters, and took off through the air.

"They told me things," he started, "but I don't remember what they said. In fact, I don't remember much of anything, but I'm sure I was there longer than only a few confusing moments."

"Days, Clem," I said. "You were there for days. Are you all right?"

"I'm bitterly hungry," he said.

"Of course. You must be starving."

"They fed me. A little. Olives and pears."

I sighed. "Thank goodness for that. Let me take you out to get food."

He smiled. "I would like that very much, Adam."

"So would I, to indulge in a mortal outing with my best friend."

He smiled, and arm in arm, we walked to that little café down the road a couple of blocks, and Clem had some very interesting things to tell me.

I had asked him to be my child, and he declined, which I

expected. It almost hurt me in a way, but in another, I loved Clem's mortality and was almost afraid of ending it.

"I think I'm ready to go home now," he said. "I'm getting tired."

"Let's then," I answered.

"Thank you. Really, Adam, for everything."

"Of course," I said, touching his shoulder. "I told you I loved you, and I meant it."

"And I believed you. I still do."

"Which is why I must ask you again, my Clem—as always."

As she stared into me, I alone could feel her age and her power. I could see the land where it all started, where Ké Hé Zule had created Verarsoe and where Lacara and her sisters had been created as well—France.

"These are secrets I am telling you," she started. "Secrets of things you must never tell another. This is the truth behind the legend, Adam. The place of my birth to darkness was France, but before I begin with my actual creation, allow me to go back in time to explain the legend of the elders.

"Ké Hé Zule was his name, as I am sure you already know."

I nodded shyly.

"His loneliness was unbearable. This man was a terrible sinner cast out by God from all human kind. Perhaps not God but by something more powerful than him.

"He was cursed with a horrifying existence that could not be ended except by the sun or fire. With his curse came an insatiable lust for human blood. He wandered the earth for many eons until at last his loneliness consumed him, and in the country of Egypt, he found a beautiful princess with hair as black as ebony—the princess Sekhmet, with eyes like the sands of the Sahara. Ké Hé Zule had secretly fallen in love with Sekhmet, watching her from afar with his vampire eyes until at last he decided to perform the evil task.

"Through his blood, he delivered to her his curse, his power, and his life. She delivered to him all her secrets, her knowledge, her dreams. Together they planned to rule the dark world. But Sekhmet was also given his evil, and obeying Ké Hé Zule was not something she had planned. Because of this, she tried to rise above him, to throw down The Father and rule alone. Ké Hé Zule knew of this but kept silent with his own secret plans. He obeyed everything Sekhmet said until at last he could endure it no longer.

"He used his superior strength to cast Sekhmet into his chamber of ice. There, she would be frozen for all eternity, to live in misery forever. But Sekhmet was powerful, more powerful than The Father could have possibly imagined. She had created in secret four sisters and destroyed their mother. My sisters and I—created by the vile Sekhmet herself!

"After being without a companion, Ké Hé Zule found a young homeless boy in the land of Egypt named Verarsoe. Verarsoe lived with Ké Hé Zule until the time came when he wanted his own underground haven and his own apprentice."

"Relone."

"Yes," she answered. "Ancient Relone. As Sekhmet lay frozen in that dreadful chamber, her fury grew in her eyes, and as this fury grew day by day, it grew to flames and melted the ice. She escaped the chamber and searched for the lover who had betrayed her. When at last she had found him, she set fire to his flesh.

"Ké He Zule was destroyed, and Sekhmet was left to rule. Before she did, she had hidden away for centuries in sorrow and misery, mourning over the loss of her ancient lover, whose very blood and evil flows through her veins."

Lacara paused, so I took the opportunity to speak. "Evil?"

"Evil." She turned away from me. "The evil from Ké Hé Zule passed into Sekhmet and each generation after her. What you do with that evil is your own choice. Not all vampires are evil, Adam, but that feeling of evil you just can't escape was released into you."

I didn't answer.

"I was only a young girl. My sisters and I were no older than sixteen years of age. I myself was fourteen.

"Screams echoed through the city that dreadful night, and fog rolled in. It hadn't snowed in France that night, and I wasn't very cold, but I concealed myself beneath the blankets of my bed for security.

"The screams in the city grew louder until they reached my very own home. The room down the hall from mine was my mother's. Strangled cries rang through the house. I sprang up in bed. I knew in an instant she was dead, and I could do nothing about it. I feared I would be next. I clenched my hands into fists. I crawled back beneath the warm blankets of my bed with my fingers in my ears, but before I was even able to calm myself, I felt cold, metal-like fingers around my throat.

"'Be silent, or I will take pleasure in killing you!' I heard. The voice was small, and my mortal ears could almost hear the vague sound of age in it. There was a sense of nervousness that her voice sent through me, but as strange as it may seem to say this, even now, there was a sense of comfort in her presence. It meant at least I was not alone. Even as the fear filled my soul—I didn't want her to leave. The strength of her fingers didn't hurt. She didn't want it to.

"I moaned a little in fear, and her grip tightened. I tried to keep silent, but I felt the whimpers of fear urging from my mouth, so I squinted my eyes shut and held my breath. At last the urge to cry out had left me, and soft tears took their place.

"She whispered her name. 'Sekhmet,' she said. 'Serve me, my child.' Though evil and deceit poured out of her, there was a sense of love she had for me.

"Now you must remember Sekhmet was more powerful than Ké Hé Zule simply because of the power she had possessed before she was made immortal. Some said she had been blessed by the Gods. Some said her father, Ashman, had put some kind of spell on her, for he was the pharaoh and one thought to have sorcery in him. There was something about Ashman the people of Egypt did not understand. To this day, I cannot tell you what it was that was so marvelous about him. My own eyes have never been set on him before.

"The Mother released into me this amazing potency I could never have imagined. I felt the pain in my neck. I knew my very blood was being drained, but I didn't know how to stop it, so I let myself weep and held very still.

"'Don't be afraid,' Sekhmet said. 'Nobody will harm you.'

"I wanted to believe her, but my fear wouldn't allow it. I could feel her cold, hard skin upon my lips now, and a hot liquid filled my mouth. It burned all the way through me, and I loved it.

"Lacara, first immortal made by The Mother. It was said she had created none, but the four sisters were her deepest secrets, and now she is back to perform a different task. So much more is held within her heart, so much more she wants and will stop at nothing to get!"

"And your sisters?"

"Yes," she answered softly. "My sisters and I wandered France alone, not ever knowing exactly what happened to Sekhmet.

"Later, we were able to read The Book of Shadows, started

by Ké Hé Zule and handed down to his apprentice, Verarsoe. Verarsoe served him well, served him like a god.

"My sisters are all I have ever really known, and I am so grateful they had not been taken away from me like my sweet, loving mother was. I miss my mother."

She sank her head low and wouldn't look at me.

"Lacara," I started, "thank you for helping me."

"There isn't really anything I can do to help you."

"I know." I squeezed the medallion in my hand and sighed. "But thank you for wanting to."

"When, Adam?" she asked softly, trying to sound strong though I knew she was afraid.

"I don't know, ma chére," I answered. "I'm sorry, love. But for now, I know you and I have a beautiful home, just you and I, with Relone just down the street."

"But what if that is all stripped away from us?" she asked.

"It won't be, Rayne."

"And why?" she yelled. "Why wouldn't it be? Why wouldn't Sekhmet tear down our homes?"

"She won't hurt you!" I yelled back, putting up my hands. "I promise you, chére. She will not hurt those I love."

"But, my darling—you love so many," she said, letting a tear fall.

I wrapped my arms around her.

Sekhmet would come soon enough, and I couldn't stop the nervous worry in the pit of my stomach. How could I stop her this time? What could I do to save myself and my family? What now? I was terrified, but I wouldn't admit it. Vanity wouldn't allow it.

I went to see Clem the next night.

"You know I will never stop asking you," I told him.

"Why is that, Adam?"

"Because I will never stop wanting you."

"As many times as you ask me, Adam, my response will be the same," he answered softly. "I will never take the blood, but I have something more to say, so don't walk away from me again."

"What do you have to say, Clem?"

"I have to say that I love you," he started. "And that I will be your companion in this life and in the life after."

"What life after?"

"I'm not finished yet."

"I'm sorry, Clem," I whispered. "Finish."

"And if there is no life after, then you will still have those memories, Adam, and I will always be with you."

"But it isn't enough," I whispered. "I love you, and I want you as my child."

He sighed. "And it would be fun for a while, but it wouldn't be right. There are no answers, are there? No reason. I do love you, Adam. I just don't want to become you."

"I know. But there really is no pain in it."

"Isn't there?"

"It was painful for me because I fought against it," I said. "I tried to force the changes out of me—and that hurt, but if you let it happen…"

"Please leave, Adam."

"Clem …"

"Please."

I sighed. "I'll stop asking you. Just please don't make me leave. Start a fire or something."

"But it isn't cold."

"Yes, but it would be nice," I argued back.

Of course, I could have lit the fire with my mind, but I wanted to watch Clem do it. He smiled, and it made me smile back. He was such an easy person to know. He didn't hold things back or hide anything at all. I wished I could have been that way.

He didn't seem like himself. I feared I frightened him. I would never hurt him—would I?

I stood up and saw him back away. I took a step forward, and he took one back. All I wanted to do was embrace him as I had done before.

"Clem, I… What's the matter?"

"I really would like it if you left," he said, "before you… take me against my will."

"Clem, I would never do that. Why would you think that?"

He didn't answer.

I sighed. "You're right. I am mean. There is meanness in me. I'll leave you now, Clem."

"I didn't mean that," he retorted. "You're not mean. You're just strong. You know what you want and will stop at almost nothing to get it!"

"No." I laughed. "You can say it, Clem. It's all right. Tell me I'm mean. I like it. I want you to tell me."

"Goodbye, Adam," he said, smiling. He wasn't angry. "You can come back tomorrow if you promise not to ask me,"

"I will ask you every night."

He sighed.

"Dio mio," I said with a sigh, stepping inside. The sun was beginning to rise, and Rayne was already asleep. I didn't wake her to let her know I was home; I just crawled into bed beside her. I hadn't fed that night, and I wondered why I wasn't hungry. Perhaps it was the power of Sekhmet that was sustaining me. I didn't want to think about The Mother. I just wanted to sleep.

"Yes, Adam," I heard Rayne whisper. "Just sleep. Don't worry your mind with such troubles." I felt her arm around my waist, and I stroked her hand. The sun was coming, and I was losing consciousness. I fell into a deep sleep, one I hadn't experienced since those lost years, and it felt good.

When I awoke, I was still tired, but I was hungry, and once I fed, the exhaustion would fade. This time it was fun. The victim basically came to me. I sat outside on a bench near the bakery; it was a cool night, almost spring in California. A young girl passed my way, staring and smiling as she walked.

"Excuse me," I called, pushing a French accent rather than Italian through my words. "You dropped this, chére," I said handing her her wallet. What a way to get a man's attention.

We ended up talking, and she asked me out for coffee. I almost felt bad leading her on so she could be my breakfast. Before we reached the café, I led her into an alleyway. What she thought I had planned was not at all what I was thinking. I took her without a sound. No frightening thoughts about me, even right before the bite. She thought she was in love already. I said a prayer for her, even though I didn't believe anybody was listening, and went home immediately to let Rayne know I had just gone out for food.

I went to see Relone afterward; I had missed him so much.

"Why do you torment yourself with this love for Clem?" he asked. "Why do you let yourself love him so much?"

"I really don't know, Relone," I answered. "I just do, and I can't help that. He's like the brother I have always wanted."

"I know what it's like to love someone, but just remember, Adam, you have Rayne, and you will always have me."

"Oh I know. I'm not looking to replace you," I said embracing him.

Clem wasn't mine yet, but I truly hoped someday he would be, and, of course, I asked him again, as I would every night thereafter.

"Do you want it, Clem, my Clem?" I asked softly. "I know you do. Just say it. Don't be afraid. No pain."

He sighed, backing away. "Adam, I…"

He backed farther away, but I came on. "Just say it," I whispered. "Don't you want it?"

"Not from you," he whispered, and through his thick Irish accent I clearly understood. "But yes—I want it."

About the Author

Sara J Bernhardt is an author and poet who has been writing since a very young age and is a winner of several poetry and short story contests. It is clear that Bernhardt writes in a realistic tone while still creating the enthralling feeling of fantasy. Her writing puts readers in a world that they will truly love to be a part of. Though the writing is edgy and catching it is also not too complex which makes it a comfortable and enjoyable read for everyone.

You can follow Sara at these locations:
Facebook
www.facebook.com/Sara-J-Bernhardt
Website
www.sjbernhardt.com

Other Works by Sara J. Bernhardt

https://books2read.com/HuntersTrilogySet

Summer's Deceit (Hunters Trilogy – Book 1): Jane Callahan is a reclusive, seventeen-year-old high school student dealing with the death of her beloved brother. Her home in Southern California with her mother is a constant reminder of her loss and pain. In hopes of escaping her past she moves to North Bend Oregon to live with her father, where she meets a beautiful boy named Aidan Summers. Jane is intrigued by his looks as well as his unusual ways of attempting to get her attention. After months of uncommon conversation and frustration, an uncertain romance brews between Jane and Aidan, but Aidan has a ghastly secret that could destroy everything.

Summer's Shadow (Hunters Trilogy – Book 2): Aidan Summers, a seventeen-year-old, stunningly beautiful genius, somehow finds his way into the life of Jane Callahan; a lovely girl trapped in soggy North Bend, Oregon. In this new Tale by Sara J. Bernhardt, Aidan relates his side of the story. All of his dark secrets are revealed and all of his motivations behind his strange ways become known as the story unravels in a captivating narrative of suspense, romance, courage...and murder.

Summer's Redemption (Hunters Trilogy – Book 3): The secret alliance of The Silver Wing and the waging war with their evil rival, The Sevren, come into full view in a new light. The evil that still lurks and stirs behind the supposed destruction of The Sevren steps out of the shadows and spins a new tale of adventure, suspense, romance, mystery and terror.

Also from the Lavish family

Irrevocable Series
Samantha Jacobey
https://books2read.com/IrrevocableSet

The end of the world is coming, or so they say, and that puts Bailey Dewitt on a crash course with Armageddon. Orphaned, she and her young brothers find themselves living with their renegade uncle as part of a group of survivalists. She struggles against them, searching for a way to escape, but every discovery only terrifies her more.

For Caleb Cross, the Ranch is a way of life. The members of their group are family, and none should come between them. Smitten from the moment he met Bailey, his choices are no longer easy, his path no longer clear. He wants to welcome her and the twins into their fold and hopes his kin will agree.

But the elders who lead them aren't interested in the trouble-some girl. They are plotting for the time they will be rid of her and expect Caleb to go along with their plans - he is after all one of them.

At first, Bailey resists Caleb's charms, but soon must admit that she desperately needs a friend. She has no intention of anything more, but when the elders make their move, she is forced to trust him with her very life.

They both have hard lessons to learn. Relationships built on secrets and lies don't come with guarantees. When the world falls apart around them, some things are Irrevocable.

www.ingramcontent.com/pod-product-compliance
Lightning Source LLC
Chambersburg PA
CBHW072230190626
46809CB00017B/1690

9781944985714